A Change of Heart

A Change of Heart

Laura Chapman

E. P. Dutton & Co., Inc. New York

LIBRARY OF CONGRESS CATALOGING IN PUBLICATION DATA

Chapman, Laura.
  A change of heart.

  I. Title.
PZ4.C4653Su3   [PS3553.H285]   813'.5'4   75–33358

Published simultaneously in Canada by Clarke, Irwin & Company
Limited, Toronto and Vancouver
ISBN: 0-525-07938-6

To my parents.

Chapter 1

There was only one passenger in the limousine, a pallid, lanky girl whose narrow form was encompassed by the folds of a dun colored dress, as wilted as she felt after passing through the grimy heat of the early stages of her trip. She was staring out of the car window, her habitually earnest gaze temporarily unseeing. Despite her length of limb, she hardly filled the corner of the broad back seat into which she had instinctively curled like a snail in a gray plush shell, a sentient snail approaching the pot, its fate written before it as clear as a recipe.

Fentiman, the chauffeur who had met her when she descended from the ferry, drove the silver-gray Rolls-Royce down a narrow dirt road under the leafy arches of a bright midsummer day, but it was dim in the blissfully cool recesses of the automobile. Tina willed the short ride to last, while she enjoyed the luxurious solitude. Soon she would again be with what was, in a sense, her family, and at Lilly Hemmingway's command as unpaid companion to her half-sister and brother, Mimsi and Goddard Mallard, to her cousins Brooke and Leigh Goddard, and to Lilly's son, Finny. The summer vaca-

I

tion was in full swing on the island, and Tina could well imagine, from past visits when her presence had been requested, that she would find herself useful to Lilly. And yet, she knew she should be grateful not to be forgotten altogether, for she had no claim to the notice, much less hospitality, of her long-dead father's second wife. For her own part, despite the grandeur of the house to which she was bidden and the supposed glory of occasional introductions to those whose names and pedigrees were heavenly harmonies to her own mother's ears, Tina would have willingly forgone this visit. Indeed, she had begged to be allowed to decline her "Aunt" Lilly's kind but unsolicited invitation. With one more year of college ahead of her before she received a degree (with what she hoped would be honors) in the archaeology of Mexico, she had planned to spend this summer working at the Zapotec site of Mitla, near Oaxaca. But, at the last, grants had failed to come through, and she was inopportunely idle when Lilly's note arrived. Vainly she suggested that a job behind the counter at Woolworth's, even for the small sum she would retain out of her weekly paycheck, made far more sense for a girl in her position than would sidling in, diffidently, amongst these "relations" whose lives were so different from her own. But her mother, tightly clinging to her absurd aspirations for Tina, had been tearfully obdurate as she rejected each of her daughter's arguments.

"It doesn't matter what other girls do, dear," she said. "You simply cannot afford to let people think of you as a file clerk or a salesgirl. People will rate you at your own evaluation. You're supposed to be so intelligent, but sometimes I don't think you have any common sense. You haven't the least inkling of what the world is really like. Take your mind off those dirty old Mexican pots and think about what kind of life you're going to have. Your trust money will stop when you're twenty-one. And, goodness knows, I can't give you any advantages on the salary I make, let alone entree into the social world they live in." Her mother sighed regretfully. A rigid coif of black hair framed her vividly painted face as she seemed to dredge deep within her for the capstone to her edifice of persuasion. She brought it forth, once more, as if it had been newly discovered by her and she was convinced by its cogency. "Right now it may not seem important to you to keep in contact with your father's family, but I know when you're my age you'll look back and see that I was right." To Tina's remonstrances she turned a deaf ear, merely continuing to overwhelm her with sheer weight of words. When Tina ultimately wavered, it was a cue for a lesson in pragmatism.

"Of course, your Aunt Lilly is planning to make use of you. Otherwise she'd never have asked you to visit. That's the way of the world. Accept it and make something of the opportunity." Mary Mallard implored, "Please go, Tina, and try to seem to belong. When you meet people, make an effort to come out of your shell. Try to smile and be friendly. The contacts you make will be useful to you."

Tina acquiesced. She was unable to shatter her mother's long-held hopes for her by any rude analysis of their general obsolescence and specific inapplicability to herself. If twenty years' intimate acquaintance with her had not proved to her mother that her hopes were ill-founded, Tina didn't suppose she would manage at this juncture to make her mother face reality.

A good look at her, Tina thought, should have long since persuaded Mary Mallard that her only daughter was not going to make the social success her mother yearned for, no matter what opportunity was thrust upon her. Tina was angular and unkempt, her light eyes looked out with earnest inquiry from under heavy brows, the whole surmounted by an uncontrollable mass of dark, curly hair which she vainly tried to skewer into order at the nape of her neck. And she was tall, far too tall, towering over her more determined mother. When she unfolded to full height, which happened rarely since she shrank visibly when adjured to hold her head up, Tina was just over six feet tall. She fully agreed with the description of herself she had once overheard Lilly give: "A great gawk, but docile enough. In fact, sometimes I think she's rather dim. But I don't mind giving her house room from time to time. That's surely more than I'm obliged to do, but as long as the family is supporting her, we may as well have her here occasionally. The mother, of course, is impossible. We knew that from the first. Even Goddard never denied that; he was glad to be rescued."

Tina's father had, by general agreement, mercifully drunk himself to death before he could further cut up his relations' peace of mind. A brief, clandestine marriage—while he was still at Yale—to Mary Higgins, a townie employed in a restaurant off-campus, had resulted in Tina. After her parents' divorce had been arranged, a small allowance for Tina's support had been paid by the trustees who controlled his money. Tina had never heard her mother voice any regrets for her father; rather, marriage to him seemed to have been simply too good an opportunity to forego. Her only apparent sorrow, tinged with reluctant admiration, was that the Mallard and Goddard families, and their lawyers, combined, had proved more adept than she in putting to practice her own utilitarian philosophy. She had been utterly foreclosed from their world, except insofar as she viewed it vicariously from her saleslady's job at Bergdorf's. She still had hopes for Tina.

After their divorce, Goddard Mallard quickly remarried. But the union with his cousin Lilly had not had the hoped-for effect of returning him to the conventional channels he had been expected to follow. However, it had borne fruit in the persons of Tina's half-sister and brother, Mimsi and young Goddard. After Goddard

Mallard's demise, Lilly had made a second marriage, incrementally more successful both socially and financially, to Findlay Hemmingway, Jr., and the obligatory heir, Findlay Hemmingway III, eventually arrived to cement this pact.

Had it not been for her mother's perseverance, Tina was convinced that her unwelcome existence would soon have been forgotten by Lilly Hemmingway, for her own father had never even recalled her to mind so far as she knew. But then, drink had erased almost everything from that slate before his early death. Mary Mallard, however, was determined and assiduous in asserting her daughter's claims to notice. As a result, when Tina reached the age at which she could be expected to be capable of making a solitary journey, she had been bidden to visit the Hemmingway ménage during the course of numerous summers.

Tina had her own pride, and one of the things upon which she congratulated herself was the ability to see her situation clearly. Her goals, though still nebulous, were as alien to her mother's unexamined but unshakeable aims for her as they were to the variegated vistas to be seen from the social promontories of those paternal relatives with whom she was entitled but reluctant to claim identity. Likewise, she knew herself to be physically unattractive and was not disposed to making an attempt to hide this reality under a veneer of artifice. She believed herself to be mentally acute, a percipient observer of the motivations of others. But she shrank from making an effort to ingratiate herself, as her mother urged. She preferred to remain apart, to be independent of the approval of others for the maintenance of her self-esteem. This, she conceded, was simple prudence in light of her objective appraisal of her own inadequacies.

So, Tina determined, she would go, this one last time. Without resenting the patronage of her family, she would make herself useful and by discharging those duties which, couched as polite requests, inevitably fell to her, she would satisfy herself that Tina Mallard was earning her keep. But she would not expect more, and she would not exert herself to court favor or intimacy. She would assert no unenforceable claims to equal room under the familial roof; she would remain a transient spectator.

They had arrived. Not at the house itself, a large relic of the past, built by her father's grandfather in the early nineteen-hundreds as a family shrine. It had been erected on the occasion of his retirement from the business of purveying to the heretofore great American unwashed the benefits of sanitary porcelain equipment, an activity he had pursued to such salutary effect that he had amassed a vast fortune. The house was set on considerable acreage, so that the trip through the grounds was itself a fair drive.

The limousine was just turning smoothly through square stone gateposts, up a pink graveled driveway, banked on one side by a brilliant array of low standing flowers, white alyssum, blue candy tuft, and pink impatiens, and shaded on the right by massive hedges of rhododendron, dark shiny leaves gleaming in the sun, blossoms now faded to a sickly mauve-tinged brown. The car came to a stop before a short flight of steps leading to a vast, crazily overgrown, stone-and-shingle dwelling containing some thirty-eight rooms. Through large bay windows at the front of the house, Tina could glimpse part of the outsized formal rooms which had been laid out for gracious entertaining. Behind them she knew were the kitchens, pantries, and laundry, in one wing, the breakfast room, sunroom, and library in another. On the second floor were the spacious bedrooms, from many of which it was still possible to catch a glimpse of the ocean despite the uncurbed growth of foliage which, in the years since the mansion's erection, had blocked what must originally have been a dazzling view. Above were

6

the almost numberless servants' quarters, no longer fully occupied and in part given over to the storage of the detritus of four generations' summer holidays.

The dwelling was used, as had been intended, only for family summers at the beach and so was still referred to by its builder's modest title, Mallard Cottage. With the porch and portico freshly limed white, the urns of pink geraniums flanking the open front door, shutters enameled white and looped back to allow the entry of summer breezes, it appeared sunny and briefly welcoming to Tina. As its builder had planned, Mallard Cottage was still the magnet which drew the Mallards and Goddards together every summer for a few weeks from their homes, scattered up and down the Eastern Seaboard and even farther afield, and reminded them of the pleasures of belonging to the family. Seeing it again, Tina felt for a moment that it might indeed have been pleasant if she, too, had a real place under this roof.

Through the open screen door came three girls younger than Tina by a few years, but a generation older in poise and assurance. Mimsi, her half-sister, was sixteen; their cousins Brooke and Leigh Goddard were twins of fifteen. As the sun shone upon them, the girls looked like three life-sized Barbie dolls to Tina. Uniformly attired in their gleaming tennis whites and carrying their rackets in neat canvas-covered presses, they were heading for the bicycles aligned in shining chrome array along the rack that flanked the left side of the front steps.

Mimsi paused as she saw Tina emerge from the limousine, impatiently push back her wind-tousled hair, and shake out her wrinkled dress, the door all the while held open for her by the impassive chauffeur.

"It's Tina! Oh, super." Mimsi greeted her half-sister with enthusiasm. "Now we can get rid of that horrid German girl."

"We're ever so glad you're here, Tina," Brooke explained. "There's going to be a dance at the Yacht Club tonight and we don't want Maria to take us. Honestly! She looks like she's straight out of *Sound of Music*. Too, too wholesome. And underneath, she's absolutely, utterly sick-making. She's a sneak."

Tina assumed the girls were resentful of some curtailment of their plans resulting from Maria's reports to Lilly. Mimsi intervened to cut short the twins' welcome.

"Darling, do run upstairs and get unpacked right away. We'll be back for dinner, but right now we have a match and we simply must tear."

Brooke touched Tina's arm. "Tina, be a sport. Make sure our jeans and shirts are up from the laundry room by dinner time, will you? We'll need them tonight and we're in such a rush. We'll see you later."

"You're looking marvelous," Tina said to the three of them before they could dash off. The three tanned faces beaming up at her were similar, in part by virtue of family relationship, but even more so in their glowing perfection. Three pairs of blue eyes, framed by center-parted long hair, tiny gold rings glowing in tanned ear lobes, skin brown against the spotless white of tennis dress, alike down to the tiny, fluffy pompoms at each heel, just bobbing over the edge of white sneakers. "Before you ride off, tell me, where is Aunt Lilly? And where are the boys?"

"Goddard's out sailing," Brooke volunteered. "Alone, of course."

"Finny's probably waiting for him down at the dock," added Leigh, "or else he's finally gone to his day camp. We don't know where Lilly is."

Leigh and Mimsi exchanged conspiratorial glances full of amusement.

"But she'll be back for cocktails by five," Leigh continued. "That is, if she doesn't stay at the beach club for a drink."

Mimsi touched Tina's elbow reassuringly. "She

knows you're coming today. After all, the car did meet you. And Hodges made up your room, across from me —the yellow room. Now we've simply got to rush. We'll see you later." The three raced off, flashes of white on glistening chrome, the spokes of their wheels visibly blurring as the slow-surfaced gravel drive gave way to the hard, packed dirt road, and the bicycles picked up speed.

Tina ascended the front steps, followed by Fentiman, who had removed her single suitcase from the trunk of the car. "I'll take this up to the yellow room then, shall I, Miss?" he asked politely, and at Tina's nod, proceeded to climb the circular staircase, hardly impeded by the slight weight of the luggage. Tina, unwilling to place total reliance on the girls' account of the whereabouts of the inhabitants, began a slow tour of the main floor.

White wicker furniture stood about the large square entry. It had been re-covered: the gay orange-and-yellow floral print she remembered had been replaced by a smart black-white geometric design. Tina strolled through the empty living room past the grand piano and peered into the brown-paneled library. The room appeared to be deserted, but Tina's ears caught a muffled noise—between a snort and a giggle—coming from the corner into which an ornate green-baize-covered pool table had been pushed. Peering between the heavy paw-like appendages of the table base she spied a grimy torn sneaker. As she stooped to look deeper into the gloom, she met the gaze of her not-quite relation.

"Finny? Why are you hiding in here?"

"Oh, hi, Tina. I thought it might be someone. Mom, or Maria, or someone. I'll come out." He ducked his head, a thatch of straw-colored hair, and scuffled out from between the massive legs of the table, then stood and leaned against it. A dusty beam of light revealed a dirty face spattered with freckles merging into less specific stains of grime. He wore the obligatory white alligator shirt and white shorts from which protruded an astounding length of bony legs.

"But why were you hiding, Finny?"

"I'm supposed to be at day camp. Tennis lesson and swimming lesson today. I'd much rather be here alone, Tina. You can't imagine how *boring* it is. I hate sports and I hate lessons."

"I see," said Tina. "Well, you don't have to hide from *me*, do you?" Let's see if anyone's in the kitchen and get a drink, shall we?"

Forbearing to clutch Finny by his dingy hand, Tina led the way back across the living room and the entry. They traversed the length of the formal dining room, Tina catching a glimpse of Finny's doubtful face, reflected from a few paces behind her in the shell-crested mirror which hung over the sideboard. They paced through the sunny breakfast room and peered cautiously into the enormous kitchen. Mrs. Chambers, the cook, was not in evidence, nor Hodges, the maid. Remembering her cousins' request, Tina thought quickly of running back to the laundry but decided that it was more important to settle Finny with a drink first.

Once two glasses of lemonade were poured from the pitcher obligingly left in the refrigerator, Tina sat down at the table in the center of the kitchen and looked at Finny sympathetically. Sometimes she thought that he felt as much of an interloper as she did in this household, although nominally he was heir to a fortune and she was only an intermittent visitor on sufferance. But an introspective nine-year-old, preceded into this family by a half-sister and half-brother too old to be his friends, Finny seemed ill at ease and withdrawn from most of the busy activities going on about him. His father was rarely present, so far as Tina had observed. And Lilly seemed to give him little of her attention once his schedule of lessons and appointments had been arranged. While Tina had often felt resentful of her own mother's centering all aspirations upon her, she could realize that the opposite situation of benign neglect might be a little too much for a young boy to weather.

"Finny, don't you have any friends at day camp?"

"Nope. They're all dumb. They think winning games is all that matters."

Tina nodded, thoughtfully. They would grow up well-adjusted to the lives which had been prepared for them. "Well, when I see your mother I'll ask her to—"

"No, gee, don't say anything to Mother. Oh, please, Tina, don't squeal."

He sounded so desperate that Tina agreed, with a sigh. First the girls, now Finny. Her young relatives inevitably expected her to conspire with them against Lilly, a role she did not relish assuming. She recalled her resolution to remain independent from the lives about her, to perform her duties efficiently, and no more. But the children's expectations were going to make this difficult. They were all too ready to rely upon her as an ally. She knew that she would be wiser to remain aloof, and not to allow herself to be drawn into these family matters.

But, in Finny's case, she'd wait and see.

Chapter 2

Tina did not see her Aunt Lilly until the family was seated in the dining room for dinner that night. Even Finny had risen to the status of the family dining table this summer. Lilly presided at the head of the table, in her husband's absence; there was no one in the place at the foot. Mimsi sat on one side of her, Goddard on the other. Then came cousins Brooke and Leigh, on opposite sides of the table. Their parents were away, on safari in Africa, she had learned. Near the bottom of the table sat Finny and Tina, looking across at each other. Maria, the "horrid" German au pair who had not suited the girls' requirements, either did not eat with the family or was not coming down that night. In her tour of the upstairs, while bringing up the clothes requested from the laundry, Tina had passed a small room in which suitcases were standing open, ready for packing. Maria's departure apparently impended, waiting only Tina's arrival. This thought was confirmed when Lilly, smiling graciously, at last addressed Tina from the head of the table.

"I *am* pleased that you arrived today, dear. You are dependable, I'm glad to say. We have had a foreign girl staying with us, but it hasn't worked, and she'll be leaving. You won't mind going to the Yacht Club party tonight with the girls, will you? It would be such a blessing."

Tina acquiesced quite willingly, for these dances were run strictly for the fourteen- to eighteen-year-olds in residence in the summer colony, and no one could expect that she participate. There would be no need to assume an anguished air of cheer in order to mask her lack of popularity. She could relax and watch, checking to see that her gay young charges did not leave the Yacht Club at the invitation of "older" men, or become acquainted with unknowns from town who might happen to drift in, or that the smoky haze which would rise toward the ceiling of the Yacht Club did not contain any pungent aura of marijuana. Lilly might expect her to do more, to steer her charges in the right directions. Lilly herself had certainly been steered. But that was a generation ago, and if Lilly had those expectations she would have to perform her own labors. Perhaps Maria had taken Lilly's instructions too literally and that's why she had come into conflict with the girls. Whatever had led to Maria's dismissal, and the ensuing summons to Tina, didn't seem important; the result was that Tina was here, and ready to commence the performance of her duties by chaperoning the girls at the dance.

Thus, Tina was able to smile brightly at Lilly and to respond, as expected, "Of course."

"Super," said Lilly. The cousins exchanged little moués at Lilly's use of their generation's word. "Tina, stay and talk with me for a few minutes after dinner. We're really quite out of touch."

Tina was surprised, but her reaction was tinged with pleasure. Perhaps, after all this time, now that she was an adult, Lilly was beginning to accept her as a person, rather than as a mistake cleverly converted into a domestic convenience.

The meal soon ended and the two women were left alone at the table.

"Let's take our coffee onto the porch, shall we?" asked Lilly, rising gracefully but smoothing back her perfectly gleaming coiffure with an uncharacteristic nervous gesture. "It will be quiet and peaceful outside." Tina had already risen to accompany her. Balancing her tiny cup in its saucer, Tina followed Lilly's delicate form into the twilight of the side porch. The sun had just set and the light was fading from the alizavin-streaked sky. The porch was screened with a dense hedge of azalea no longer in flower. The twilight air was redolent with the scent of vernal herbage, the darkness emphasizing the mood of privacy Lilly seemed to want for their conversation. The only sound which broke the stillness was the zap of moths, committing suicide as they dove headlong into the golden glow of the insect lights which ornamented the porch railing. Tina wondered what was to come as she sat beside Lilly and rested her coffee on a small wicker stool. Lilly, seeming unsure of how to begin now that they were alone, fumbled for a cigarette and lighter.

"Tina, you look more and more like your father—as I remember him, that is." She paused, at a loss for a transition to the still unknown point of this tête-à-tête which she had sought. Tina thought, she really has something to say and she doesn't know how to put it. She's nervous at talking to me, of all people. "I'm glad you're here, now," Lilly continued, hesitating once again as she drew near to revealing the subject which was on her mind.

Tina could only sit in silence, gazing at Lilly's profile illuminated in silhouette by the faint light coming through the windows in back of them. Lilly suddenly looked very much like her own daughter, though every contour and feature was subtly sharpened and refined by age. Her fair hair was drawn smoothly into a gleaming twist on her neck, her earrings large hoops engraved to imitate golden shrimp. The skin glistened over the high arch of her forehead and the slight aquilinity of her nose. But her appearance of enameled perfection was belied by the unease of her gestures as she sought, for the first time that Tina could remember, to communicate with her.

The wicker chair in which Tina was ensconced creaked beneath her as she shifted position to relieve the tension building in her. Yet she was glad that they were both sitting. It would be easier talking to Lilly in this position than looking down from her usual towering vantage point. Perhaps Lilly had considered this.

"Tina, it may surprise you that I should choose to take you into my confidence. But you seem to be very mature and, after all is said and done, we must consider you to be a member of the family. I'm alone in this house, in charge of it and everyone within it. My husband is abroad once again, traveling on a mission for his foundation. In any event, I don't expect that he'll come to the island this summer. My brother and sister-in-law are in Africa as well, on safari somewhere in Tanzania. I've been left with all the responsibility." Her voice was slightly tinged with bitterness. "Recently, I've become worried." She drew a breath. "This girl, Maria, was supposed to be a godsend. She came with the highest recommendations, but almost from the first the girls have complained about her. I thought they simply resented her way of exerting authority—they're not quite children any longer—and perhaps her manner was a little more severe than what they've been accustomed to. They give them so much liberty at school nowadays that when they are at home on holiday it can be a bit difficult to cope. Anyway, it seemed that we'd have no peace this summer as long as Maria was with us. Luckily, I thought of you. As soon as you said you would come I discharged her. But when I informed Maria that I would no longer require her services, she told me to my face that it would be worth my while to keep her and that I had better make it worth hers to stay! It was really unpleasant." Lilly shuddered slightly.

Tina could well believe that so untoward a reaction from one of her servants would have struck Lilly as more than unpleasant. It was doubtful that anyone else in her employ had ever failed to acquiesce promptly to her wishes. Still, it did seem that she was dwelling on this scene with more than normal intensity. Tina would have expected it to become part of the currency of island conversation, an important portion of which at any given time consisted of the tribulations endured by the summer colonists at the hands of those who were being paid—handsomely mind you—to perform services that were all too often deemed inadequate when rendered. Maria's effrontery, Tina thought, would merely have provided additional value to this anecdote in the retelling. Yet Lilly was relating it as a grim experience and had insisted on doing so in strictest confidence. It was uncharacteristic.

Lilly finished her coffee and put aside the cup. "Naturally, I couldn't consider keeping her for a moment after that. But I am concerned. She was obviously trying to blackmail me into letting her stay, and into paying well for the privilege. She implied that I would know why. But of course I don't—except that, according to Mimsi, she has been snooping about everywhere in this house for the best part of a month. I certainly don't know what, if anything, she thinks she's discovered that would be useful as a threat. And I will not see her again, under any circumstances. But I want you to be alert, Tina. If there is . . . if there should be anything that comes to your notice which you think I should know about, you must tell me at once."

Tina stared at Lilly, even more perplexed. While Lilly denied any knowledge of a basis for Maria's vague threat, she was surely overreacting to it. But then it was sufficiently odd in and of itself that Maria should be so very anxious to keep her job at Mallard Cottage. Knowing Lilly, Tina doubted there was any very munificent salary attached to it and as Tina was well aware, although the job was not very onerous, it lacked compensating attractions. The whole scene, as recounted by Lilly, as well as Lilly's reaction to it, was certainly strange enough, but hardly, Tina would have thought, sufficient to cause Lilly to turn to her in the equality of an alliance.

Tina decided to minimize the situation. "But surely you misunderstood her. Perhaps her English isn't very good, Aunt Lilly. You may have read too much into her outburst. Or she may merely have wanted to indicate that she liked the job and wanted to stay on. You surely don't think that there's anything really wrong here?"

"No," Lilly replied at once, as if she had already dismissed these explanations in her own mind. "I haven't imagined anything. Her words and manner were absolutely insolent. I want her out of here as soon as possible. I had to tell you about her threat because, if there is anything at all to it, and you learn of it, I am relying on you to inform me immediately. Once I know, of course I will have our lawyers deal with her."

"But do you suspect anything, Aunt Lilly? Otherwise, I don't quite see why . . . or rather, what there is to worry about."

Lilly seemed momentarily annoyed at Tina's response. But then she made an effort at a laugh and said, "You're probably quite right. I don't really believe there's any substance to this. With Findlay away, and so much on my mind, I suppose I've inflated this little unpleasantness out of all proportion. There, you see? I was quite right to discuss it with you. I feel much easier already. I'm sure there really is nothing to worry about. When I put it into words, it did sound ludicrous, didn't it? Well, then, dismiss the whole thing from your mind, and so shall I."

Turning her gaze from the darkness of the night outside Lilly smiled with conscious charm, and changed the subject. "But so far our conversation has been all about us. You must tell me, Tina, what has your year been like? You're studying . . . art, isn't it? How have you been getting on?"

Tina nodded and accepted her cue. "Not art, actually, archaeology—the early civilizations of Mexico. There are relatively few written records in existence, but there are literally millions of artifacts already excavated which still must be dated and collated, and their inscriptions deciphered. I'd hoped to work at a field site this summer, on a project studying the artifacts of the Zapotecs. Then I would have had material for my honors thesis. But, my job fell through." Tina smiled wryly. "So here I am."

"Well, we must be glad of it." Lilly's reply was determinedly gracious. "Although, had you asked Findlay to use his influence, I imagine something could have been arranged. But why should you study so hard all summer? If it interests you, it's all very well to learn about it in school, I suppose. But what good will it do you in the long run? You'll be getting married and it won't matter then if you've finished an honors paper or not."

"You sound just like my mother," Tina said before she thought.

Lilly stiffened perceptibly. "Really!"

Tina realized her mistake and was flooded by embarrassment. "I think I'd better go upstairs and collect the girls for the dance now, Aunt Lilly," she stammered.

"Yes, you'd best do that," Lilly replied coolly, their confidential relationship at an end for the time being.

"Will Goddard be coming too?" Tina inquired.

"Oh, Goddard! I doubt if he'll be interested in a dance at his age. He's only fourteen, after all. But keep an eye on the girls. I'm going to be playing bridge at the Wigmores'. And I've got a golf match at the club tomorrow morning. So I'll probably see you at dinner, if I'm in.

Good night, Tina." Lilly's dismissal was quite in her usual manner.

Tina fled from Lilly's presence. What could have possessed her? Her mother and Lilly were very much alike in their attitudes but it was fatal to compare them. She raced upstairs, her embarrassment having almost driven Lilly's peculiar confidence from her mind. But she was brought to a pause outside the room which had apparently belonged to Maria. The door was ajar and the lights on, and the suitcases were now closed, standing on their spines. She gave way to temptation and peered in, only to find as she passed over the threshhold that this time the room was occupied.

But it was not a young woman whose startled gaze met hers; it was her half-brother Goddard who stared up at her from his seat on the edge of the bed.

"Why, Goddard, what are you doing here?"

"I want to talk to Maria," he said, shortly.

Tina was mildly surprised, but replied lightly, "Did you? Well, she's plainly not here and I don't think you ought to be waiting in her room, do you?"

He sighed and then preceded her out of the room, mutely, and she closed the door firmly behind them. Goddard continued down the hall ahead of her until, entering his own room, he slammed the door shut.

Tina shook her head. Her relations with Goddard had always been a bit uneasy. Mimsi and her cousins had always seemed glad to accept her at face value, pleased with the assistance she rendered them in facilitating their plans. But Goddard's reaction to her had always been different. Of course, Tina reminded herself, there was little that she could do for him; he seemed quite independent. Their general awkwardness with each other she attributed to her own inexperience with boys, of any age, and to the obvious ambiguities in their kinship status which seemed troublesome to her half-brother. Had it not been for her conversation with Lilly, she wouldn't have given Goddard's odd conduct another thought. Anyway, she would have to hurry now to dress for her role as chaperone at the Yacht Club Juniors' Fortnightly Dance.

Chapter 3

The Yacht Club, a simple white frame building half extending over the waters of the harbor, dominated the center of the village. Though unprepossessing from the outside, it remained a focal point of social life on the island. No attempt had been made to "decorate" it; it was the Yacht Club as it had always been, and there was no need to attract new members. It was spacious though spartan within, and ample decks on the water side made it an ideal location for a small, informal dance.

Tina sat in a faded red-and-white canvas chair, which she was grateful to have found vacant, even though it was somewhat too near the loudspeaker. If her more advanced age and greater height had been insufficient to set her apart, she concluded that her wardrobe alone would have done so. She was dressed neatly—and she had believed unobtrusively—in a simple navy cotton shirtwaist. Her face was scrubbed clean and her errant hair, affected as ever by the damp sea air, was nevertheless dutifully restrained, she hoped, by bobby pins and elastic. Comparing herself with those in the throng before her, she was struck by the fact that the attire she had thought innocuous enough to camouflage her presence instead served to mark her as an interloper.

Genuine Levis worn with elaborately embroidered work shirts were definitely the current uniform. This might well be standard all over the country, she thought. The current dress fads seemed to be adopted with miraculous speed, donned faithfully until the mysterious signal for the next costume change was picked up by the group antennae. But to Tina's half-trained eye, there was an even more unmistakable identity about the members of the group before her. The unmixed dolichocephaly, the surely remarkable persistence of post-infantile blondism amongst these long-haired teenagers made her feel that she was in the presence of a coherent tribal group, rather than an admixture of youth from the cities and towns of the East Coast, from further reaches such as Dallas and Cleveland, and from the more exclusive suburbs of Chicago and Detroit. Even in their seniors she saw the homogeneity of these traits, even more marked in some cases, since to long-headedness were added long, narrow jaws resulting in a somewhat toothy appearance. Not the broad, flashing, white-toothed grins of dairy-fed second-generation Scandinavians, but the result of teeth crowded forward into overly narrowed orbits, which gave even to those who were mature, but not superannuated, a claim to be called "long in the tooth." How could this cast of countenance have become indigenous to what was, after all, a resort subject to a fluctuating population each summer? Only an analysis of the intricate family relationships amongst these returnees from scattered geographic locations—an intricacy illustrated by her own family's mingling of Goddards and Mallards, with the occasional addition of Hemmingways or Wigmores—could explain the fixing of these traits in the current crop of descendants. Indeed, as much as Mimsi and her cousins resembled each other, there were half a dozen other lithe girls on the floor who might have laid equal claim to kinship if appearance was the test.

Chin in hand, Tina watched the youngsters vibrate to the music blaring over the loudspeaker. One or two parents passed through the crowd without lingering, the requisite bow to traditions of chaperonage she supposed. But none of the kids seemed to be under the permanent eye of an older person. Different as the mores of this class might be from the rest of the country, still the strict traditions which might have yet prevailed when Lilly was an adolescent, seemed long since to have been dropped by everyone else. Why should she still be insistent that the girls, at least, be closely watched? It was strangely out of keeping with Lilly's general attitude toward her children, which was, so far as Tina had observed, heavily leavened with relief when they were out of sight. The three girls were certainly old enough now to get down to the club and back on bicycles like the rest of the crowd. But even if Lilly preferred to have them delivered and picked up by the car, why did she feel the need to have them supervised once they had safely arrived?

Then her thoughts were interrupted. She was being addressed. Glancing up, she saw there was after all one other individual present who was at least her own age— and, as she quickly observed, height.

"I said I haven't seen you here before."

Tina looked up, past white ducks and a faded denim shirt, as she rapidly inspected the young man unaccountably talking to her. He reminded her, briefly, of an older Finny suddenly elongated to an extreme, as he stared down at her from behind the horn rims of his eyeglasses. But then her relatives shared a family resemblance with half the people she met on the island. As he continued to look her over, Tina lost sight of her initial reaction. This young man's calculating appraisal of her possibilities was extremely annoying. He was waiting coolly for her to explain herself, to justify her existence to him. So there was an edge to her voice when she said, "No, that's right, you haven't seen me before. I've only just come out to stay at Mallard Cottage."

"I wondered. You're much too old to be here for the dance."

"Yes, quite," she replied, unconsciously adopting Lilly's tone.

"I didn't mean to be rude," he said, more in explanation than apology, and proceeded, unabashed by her dismissive manner. "I just wondered why you're here. I'm working at the Yacht Club for the summer and there aren't many—I mean, everyone our age seems suddenly to disappear from the island and not to reappear until they return with their first baby."

She forced herself to smile in acknowledgment of the justice of his observation. Perhaps his unwelcome approach might be redeemed by some spark of interest in his conversation. And, after all, he didn't seem too terribly daunting. He did not strike her as being unbearably suave nor obviously superior. "Yes, you're right," she replied less defensively. "I've noticed that myself. Well, I'm visiting and it was *requested* that I accompany the girls. So here I am."

"Oh, then are you Maria's replacement?" he asked.

"You might say that," she answered. "I'm Tina Mallard."

"Tina *Mallard?*" He repeated her name, emphasizing the last syllables. There was more surprise in his reiteration than Tina enjoyed hearing. "And I'm Tony Corbin. Funny we haven't met before. I mean, last year, or before," he added vaguely.

Yes, I know just what you mean, Tina thought. You can't quite place me as a Mallard and you think you should be able to. "Yes, funny," she agreed as equably as she could. "How do you come to be working on the island for the summer?"

"I had to have some sort of job. I'm in charge of the

24

Yacht Club. General housekeeper and giver of sailing lessons. It's not too bad, but of course there's no one over sixteen around to talk to most of the time. I was beginning to wonder if I could hold out until the end of the season."

"And then?" Tina inquired.

"Oh, back to Dartmouth. Pre-med. I've one more year."

"I can't believe it," she exclaimed. Then realizing how rude her remark must have sounded, she attempted to explain. "You're the first younger person I've ever heard of on this island who wasn't hoping to get into, or stay in, Hollins or Rollins. Someone could surely make a fortune by laying on a stable and tennis courts and starting a new post-nursery school—called 'Collins,' of course."

"You do sound superior," he replied. "And where do *you* go to school? Not Hollins, or Rollins, or even Finch, I presume," he inquired with amusement.

"No, not Finch, nor Pine Manor. And I admit it, I did sound condescending. I've finished my junior year at Hunter. It's a college in New York City, you know. And I am interested in what I'm studying, which seems to strike most people here as rather odd."

"Then put me down as one of the odd ducks, too. Playing squash and managing money didn't appeal to me as a life's work. I've had a hard time convincing my family that I really mean to become a doctor."

Tina attempted to smile encouragingly up at him. "Sit down, can't you?" she invited. When he hesitated she stiffened. "Or are you too busy?"

"Well, I'd better keep moving," he replied. "They're filing in and out, smoking, and I have to make sure that no one sets fire to the cushions on the lounges or throws any furniture off the deck."

Tina quickly resumed her former manner. "I see you bear weighty responsibilities," she commented dryly.

"That reminds me. I'd best check on my charges. My Aunt Lilly seems to be strangely concerned about them so I'd best stroll around and make sure they're not up to anything."

As Tina rose to her feet she saw him start, and thought she saw the glimmerings of amusement imperfectly concealed by the lenses of his tortoise-shell glasses. Standing next to him, she was fully his height.

Tony Corbin's momentary reaction had been caught and he knew it. "Well, I certainly couldn't have run into you before and forgotten it, Tina. You're overwhelming," he said and laughed, as much at himself as at her.

Tina blushed. "And *you* are offensive. I thought so when you first came over, and now I'm sure of it. Don't they include instruction in rudimentary manners anymore in your expensive and exclusive boarding schools?"

Tony smiled at her fury. "Okay, I won't make any more cracks about your height, but you know, you're really much too sensitive. Let's both get back on the job. I'll be seeing you around," he called over his shoulder as he left her standing there.

Tina turned aside, smoldering. For a moment he had seemed so nice, so different from the usual run of men she had observed on the island. Not too young, not old and married, or divorcing. Not too sports mad to be devoid of conversation. Perhaps someone with whom she could occasionally exchange a congenial word. And he was, after all, just a Yacht Club employee so she would not have had to condemn herself for opportunism if they had become friendly. But once he'd seen that she was almost as tall as he, he couldn't resist trying to—well—belittle her. She'd manage to keep out of his way for the rest of the summer, which didn't seem as if it would be too hard to do.

After checking on Brooke and Leigh and Mimsi, all happily dancing with or against partners in the middle of the floor, Tina was unprepared for the sight of Goddard, who was standing in a crowd by the punch table. She made her way over to him. Before she could speak, he said, "It was too quiet at home. Everyone's out, so I decided to drop in and take a look around."

Tina thought to herself, what about Finny, and the staff? Someone was always supposed to be in the house. But, perhaps Goddard didn't count them as anyone. "I think it's nice that you've come," she said finally. "You'll see all your friends, and the music is terrific. Why don't you ask one of the girls to dance?"

Goddard ignored this suggestion. "I saw you talking to Tony Corbin. He's a great sailor."

"No. Really?" she said, sounding unimpressed.

"God, yes. He's ranked," he explained in an awed voice. Since Tina looked blank, Goddard added, "Nationally. He won the Sears Bowl a couple of years ago. That's the national championship for juniors, you know. It's just great that they got him to take on the Yacht Club this year."

"Does he give you lessons?" Tina asked, amused at the fact that Tony Corbin was so obviously a hero to Goddard.

"No. But sometimes he lets me help around the club. Getting the Sunfish in and stacked, going over sails, things like that. And I pick up tips from him. Of course, he's awfully busy."

"Is he, though?" Tina wondered if his job could actually keep the cocksure Tony Corbin on the jump. She'd like to come down to the Yacht Club one afternoon after all, to observe at her leisure the prospect of Tony Corbin hustling around in a sweat—if it ever really happened, which she doubted. The conversation, which had been initiated and maintained largely by Goddard, a rarity, was now at a standstill. Tina felt obliged to continue it, so unusual did she find the semblance of even casual friendship between herself and Goddard, so she asked him the first question that came into her head. It had been lurking there for the last two hours.

"How did you get along with Maria, Goddard? Are you sorry that she's left?"

"Left? You don't mean she's gone?" he responded, looking shaken.

"Oh surely you knew that. Lilly fired her. She told us Maria was going when we were at dinner tonight. Weren't you listening? When I met you in her room I saw that her suitcases were shut; I presume she's moved out by now if she wasn't in the house when you left it."

"Oh, you mean that she's moved out of the cottage," Goddard stated, much relieved. "I knew that. But she said that she'd be staying on the island for a while."

"She did?" Had Lilly known this? "You seemed upset to think that she'd gone away. Did you like her?" Tina asked.

"Oh, she wasn't so bad, once you got to know her," Goddard replied evasively.

"And did you? Get to know her?"

"Oh, sort of—say, I see some guys I know out on the deck. I think I'll get some air." And Goddard escaped quickly onto the dark deck where, by peering through the doorway, Tina could see him join three other figures engaged in propping up the south elevation of the Yacht Club. So much for Goddard and the spirit of the dance, she thought. But I suppose he must be changing for the better considering that he actually spoke to me for a few minutes without being cornered. Still, it does seem odd that he's the only one at Mallard Cottage with a kind word for Maria.

He was, after all, her own half-brother even though she had somehow fallen into the habit of considering him as entirely Lilly's child. Certainly she found it easier to get along with Mimsi, who also shared their common parent. Could it be that the awkwardness with others, the preference for solitude which made it so hard to communicate with Goddard, was an inheritance from their father whom she had never known? An inheritance in which she also partook? Could such personality traits be hereditary or was she imagining things, and Goddard merely a typical adolescent boy even now emerging from an awkward stage.

Her reflections had so absorbed her that when Tina once again focused on the dance floor she was surprised to find that Brooke and Mimsi were no longer gyrating before her. An absurd feeling of panic struck her. The ladies' room? But, really, she wasn't a jailer. What did Lilly expect to happen? Still, she took another look out front and thought that she made them out in a small group near the gangplank leading down to the shore. She'd better check, she supposed.

Her approach went quite unnoticed; the four girls' heads were close together, totally absorbed. And there were Brooke and Mimsi, with two other girls their own age, giggling in a huddle. And, of course, a cigarette was being passed around. Duty called. Tina answered.

"Look girls, I know your parents don't want you to smoke."

Brooke looked up at her innocently. "Aunt Lilly smokes. Don't be a stiff. We all do."

"Well, not in front of me, anyway. Really, you don't want to get into that filthy habit. And it'll be bad for your tennis game."

"Not this kind," Mimsi asserted, asking provokingly, "Don't you want a puff?"

"Yes, I think I do." Tina took the stealthily proffered cigarette, inhaled, and, to the girls consternation, stamped it out and kicked it off the gangplank into the waters below. "Now where did you get this, Mimsi? Don't you know it's illegal? Why, you could go to jail, and the Yacht Club could be shut down if the police found you smoking this. Haven't you any sense?"

"Don't be dim, Tina. We've been smoking for absolute

years. If you haven't tried it, don't knock it," Mimsi answered with bravado.

"Oh, for pity's sake, Mimsi, and Brooke, and you girls, too. You could get into serious trouble for this."

They stared at her, incredulous. "Nobody would bother *us*, Tina."

She thought to herself, they're probably right, too. No policeman on this island is going to check into marijuana at a Yacht Club junior dance. And they probably have been smoking at school. But where in the world are they getting it? She said firmly to them, "No more. And, much as I hate to squeal, this is something Lilly has to be told." And not just Lilly she suddenly thought. Where in hell was Tony Corbin, now. She wheeled, re-entered the clubhouse, and immediately spotted him at the foot of the stairs, holding court for his young admirers. The circle was predominantly nubile. Goddard, she noted, was an absent worshipper. Well, here was some genuine work for the officious and offensive Mr. Corbin to do.

Brushing past the girls who were adoring him, she said, "If you'll excuse me, I would like to talk to you, alone."

"I didn't think my vast powers of attraction extended to you Tina." He grinned back at her, obviously enjoying the fact that she'd had to cut him out of a harem to speak with him.

"You're right, they're nil as far as I'm concerned," she answered with asperity. "But you do represent some kind of authority here. I mean, you are technically in charge, aren't you?"

"Yes, you could say that," he admitted.

"Well, my cousins and some other girls were just smoking pot outside the front door."

"Was it any good or didn't you sample it?" he asked, quite unperturbed.

"Don't you believe me? Aren't you going to do anything?" she demanded.

"What do you want me to do? Ask them all to turn out their pockets? They'd laugh in my face!"

"But surely, knowing its illegal, you have an obligation . . ." Her voice trailed off.

"Look, Tina, I'm not a scoutmaster. I just make sure they don't set fire to the furniture."

"That's disgusting," she replied in a voice revealing more outrage than she had expected. "Haven't you any sense of moral obligation, of responsibility?"

"To whom?" he asked. "Their parents? They know, or would if they didn't want not to," he retorted.

"Well, I'm going to take my charges home now. Let me use the phone. I'll call for our car."

"Somehow, I don't think you're going to remain very popular with the younger set on this island, Miss Mallard. Nor, for that matter, with the older set, if you go about stirring up a stink."

"Popularity, of that sort, doesn't concern me in the least, Mr. Corbin." Tina's eyes flamed.

"Yes, that's obvious, isn't it. Well, at least you're *big* enough to take what's going to be dished out."

Tina lost her temper. "Meaning what? That I'm so tall, I'm a freak? That I don't have any feelings? Well I do, but they include a feeling of responsibility, obviously missing from your makeup. Now, where is that phone? The sooner we're out of here, the better I'll like it—in all respects."

"Your servant, madame," he said, indicating a telephone on the wall. "I'll even lend you a dime, and bid you and your fair wards goodnight."

Tina was ushering the protesting trio into the Rolls, driven by the ever impassive Fentiman, when she suddenly remembered Goddard. "Hold on a minute. And don't you dare get out of the car, girls. I'll be right back." She dashed through the door and managed to maneuver across the dance floor and out the door to the decks without confronting Tony Corbin. But when she scouted the outer precincts of the Yacht Club and the lounging figures talking in groups out on the deck, Goddard was nowhere to be seen. Shrugging helplessly, Tina made her way back to the car.

It soon discharged them onto the front steps of Mallard Cottage, a dim bulk in which only the central lights of downstairs and upstairs halls still burned.

"Okay. That's it," she addressed them, as they sullenly made their way upstairs. "I know you're mad. I've treated you like babies and embarrassed you in front of your friends—I've gotten the message. Now let's go to bed. We'll talk about it tomorrow—with your mother, if I can find her."

Shrugging into her own nightgown a few minutes later in the privacy of the yellow room which had been assigned to her, Tina reflected that it had been quite a beginning to a six weeks' stay at Mallard Cottage. Not quite what her mother had had in mind. Or Lilly either. Unless . . . But Tina couldn't really answer her own half-formulated question until she resolved one further problem in her own mind. Was Lilly merely an older version of those vacuous charmers, her sweet young relations, or was there a chance that there was a lot more to Lilly than had, as yet, met Tina's eye?

Chapter 4

Sunlight streaming through curtains Tina had forgotten to draw the night before wakened her to the still of early morning. Anticipating with no pleasure at all the inevitable conflicts which this day would bring, Tina nevertheless rose and dressed, hoping for a quiet breakfast time in which to prepare herself for the day. But when she descended to the breakfast room, there was Lilly, immaculate in matching pink golf shirt and culottes. She sat imbibing coffee over the remains of her toast.

"Good morning, Aunt Lilly," Tina began brightly.

"Oh, do call me Lilly. You're old enough to make what was at best a courtesy title seem a bit aging to me, Tina. I'd rather it was just Lilly, in future."

"Oh, yes, fine." Tina was unsure if this was intended to further their new relationship or a way to put her at a greater distance from the veritable Mallards. "I think I must be rather high on the girls' hate list this morning, Lilly. You see—"

"Yes. I know all about it," Lilly cut her revelation short. How could she already have been informed of last night's events, Tina wondered. It was unlike the girls to stir in the morning, unless one of them had waited up last night to see Lilly? Still, that would have been rather late.

Lilly finished sipping her coffee and pushed the cup aside. "Don't worry about the girls. You did the right thing. Smoking in front of the Yacht Club, anyone could have seen them. That sort of thing can ruin a girl even years later. It won't do to let any of them get a name for wildness. So I'm awfully relieved that you removed them before notice was taken. I'm glad you were so alert and I'm very pleased with you."

Tina wasn't sure that Lilly's informant had filled her in on the entire situation. "Oh I wouldn't have made a big thing just about smoking," Tina said. "But it was marijuana, you see."

"Yes. Quite." Lilly folded her napkin and quickly passed over this news—if it was news to her. "As I said, I'm glad you were there and your actions have my full approval. It's time they showed a little sense. Brooke and Leigh are only fifteen, but Mimsi has got to start looking after herself. I'm really disappointed in her. Oh God, look at the time—I've got to dash," she said, rising. "Fentiman is dropping me at the golf club. If the girls don't need anything this morning, you can have the car. Why not do some shopping in the village? Charge what you like to me—within reason, of course." Lilly's smile was intended to be reassuring. "For goodness' sake, don't worry, Tina. They'll have forgotten all about it by this afternoon and you'll all be friends again. See if I'm not right."

The louver door flapped behind Tina. Lilly had left.

Tina sat, bemused and a bit deflated. Well, it was nice to know that she had done the right thing—if for all the wrong reasons. And a shopping trip to the village had been offered to her—a chance to acquire a few sweaters, a new pair of slacks, all within reason. Had this offer been made purely out of generosity, or could it have been intended as a distraction? In either case, Tina was willing to take Lilly up on it. Not that there was any reason for her to fuss over her wardrobe, and yet something impelled Tina to see if there might not be some outfits more in keeping with the casual mode of dress on the island.

Lilly's reaction still puzzled Tina. She was an enigma. Last night Tina had supposed that Lilly's insistence on the girls being chaperoned by her at the dance was based on some suspicion that drugs might be in circulation amongst the younger set. But if that were the case, her reception of Tina's confirmation of such suspicions had been very calm, almost uninterested. Tina concluded that she was as far as ever from understanding Lilly.

Superficially, Lilly Hemmingway's life on the island seemed to be a very pleasant one, but could she really enjoy it—coming here, every June, year after year, opening the big house and acting as hostess to any and all of the acknowledged relations who might choose to be house guests, seeing the same old faces year after year, the same people with whom she had grown up, pursuing the same avocations and amusements, tennis, golf, and cocktails with the same unswerving devotion another might give to more productive pursuits? Lilly looked as marvelous as ever, but still Findlay Hemmingway, her husband, was almost never here with her—not that anyone seemed to miss him. Perhaps they all found it more comfortable without him. Findlay Hemmingway's personality was not unobtrusive: whenever he was present, everyone seemed to be scurrying to keep out of his way before he could lay down the law to them. There was certainly a more relaxed atmosphere in the house when he was not in it. Lilly, however, might have been expected to miss him, despite the fact that she was engulfed by her friends and her social activities. Could she really be as contented as she seemed? Could anyone skim through life as lightly as Lilly appeared to do, refusing to delve beneath the pleasant surface, always relying on others to deal with any harsh or unpleasant reality? Lilly seemed to have mastered the art of living graciously, but Tina found herself wondering whether it always worked, even for Lilly.

The entrance of young Finny, another early riser, put an end to her speculations.

"Are you going to camp this morning, or would you like to come with me to the village?" Tina asked.

"Oh, I'm too busy today. Tuesday's a riding day," he told her with satisfaction.

"And you don't mind riding lessons?"

"No, that's different. Horses aren't just some dumb game," Finny explained.

Tina nodded, well satisfied. At least Finny did have one summer pursuit which he enjoyed. It had been disquieting to think of him lurking inside the shadows of the cottage all summer.

"By the way, Finny, Goddard told me last night that nobody was at home when he left. Isn't one of the maids supposed to stay in with you? I don't like to think of the house left open and all of the servants out with you here all alone."

"Oh sure, there's always supposed to be someone here."

"Was it Hodges last night or Mrs. Chambers?"

"Gee, I don't know. They don't put me to bed any more. Besides, I took a bike ride last night after supper and then turned in. I didn't see anyone."

"You mean you go out at night and nobody knows?" Tina was startled.

"Oh, don't get in a fuss. What's the difference?" said Finny.

But Tina thought there was quite a difference between Lilly's watchful regard for the girls and her apparent indifference to the whereabouts of her two young sons. And weren't children of his age supposed to be in bed at a certain hour? Goddard, she supposed might be considered old enough to be given a loose rein, but Finny, only nine, seemed already emancipated. If Lilly didn't concern herself, what about her husband?

"Have you heard from your father, Finny?" Tina asked.

"Oh, sure. He always sends me postcards so I can collect the stamps. He's touring Africa now."

"Do you know anything about this mission he's gone on? I've never really learned what your father's foundation does."

"He works for Friends of the Forest. They're saving the jungle and savanna for the preservation of African wildlife. Then the twins' parents will have something to go on safari to shoot, you see. It all works out."

"Yes," Tina replied thoughtfully, "when you put it that way it all seems to work very well. Will he be meeting your aunt and uncle, then?"

"Oh, I don't know. Africa's a big place, you know. The cards I've gotten were from Morocco and Libya. That's way up north. The safari's going to Tanzania."

Tina agreed that it was unlikely that their paths would cross. But, she thought to herself, is there any jungle or savanna in Morocco or Libya? Still, there might well be some endangered species in the North African deserts. Anyway, it was nice that he remembered to send Finny postcards. Was Lilly equally well remembered?

Her breakfast was finished and, none of the girls having appeared, she decided to make an early start for the village. She could dispense with Fentiman's services. It was a bright day and the morning air was still invitingly crisp. Perfect for a bike ride. Even if she could find anything to fit her in the few exclusive shops that had branch stores on the island, there would have to be alterations, so she could have the packages delivered.

Selecting the largest of the bicycles from the rack—a man's bike—she pedaled down the curving driveway and onto the empty road toward the village.

Chapter 5

The little village faced the harbor. A few women's shops, a drugstore and a gourmet grocery, a store that sold boating supplies, a coffee shop, and a gas station comprised the center of such town life as the island afforded. There were no restaurants, bars, or pizzerias or any facilities which might cater to the needs of tourists; the islanders preferred not to extend too much of a welcome to outsiders. The village was there strictly for their needs and no one grudged the long boat ride to the mainland towns when goods not available locally were required. It might be inconvenient, but the lack of services kept the tourists at bay, so it was worth it.

Located in an exposed position near the water, and dependent on summer residents for their trade, the stores shut down after Labor Day, and were boarded up until the next season. But, in midsummer, they were thriving, and their artfully decorated windows presented a tempting array of carefully collected luxuries.

Emerging from the second shop which she had tried, the Sea Shell Boutique, Tina decided ruefully it was unlikely she would find a discreetly colored pair of slacks on the island which could be lengthened to the top of her ankles, let alone a demure skirt. Lilly's intended treat had backfired; the sight of Tina's angular limbs protruding from garments in unwonted shades of tangerine and peacock had not been encouraging. For one who viewed clothing as a means of camouflage, the casual attire stocked in the village had been far too flamboyant. She would be better suited with what she had brought with her than by the blazing colors and revealing lines of the garments which had been proffered. Looking up from her introspection, Tina thought she saw Tony Corbin strolling down the narrow pavement in her direction; the glare of the sun directly in her eyes made it impossible to be certain. Without hesitating she ducked into the comparative gloom of the coffee shop next to the boutique. Peering out through the plate-glass window, she saw she had been mistaken. The man was quite a bit older than Tony, and even taller. His silhouette against the bright sunlight had deceived her.

Once inside she felt impelled to sit at the counter and at least order some coffee. Probably the waitress wouldn't have thought twice about it, if she had bobbed in and out of the restaurant but, as always, Tina was aware of the awkward appearance she might present.

She was the only customer in the place. The summer regulars called it "the Kraut's," although it bore on its striped canopy outside the more proper legend, "Blue Danube Coffee Shop." The owner was Max, and the name by which the shop was known derived from his obvious ancestry.

The waitress, who had been at the rear of the store busily drying glasses, came toward her with a gleaming smile to take her order. Tina couldn't help staring at her. Her golden braids were wound in two rolls over her ears; she had round blue eyes, a snub nose, and a lightly freckled rosy complexion. She was small and rather buxom, and her orange uniform was strained over each protrusion in her frame. Not Rubens, but perhaps Renoir might have taken this girl for a model. But, there was an air of shyness about Renoir's nudes. This girl was not so encumbered. Her gaze was direct and an automatic smile flashed as she asked if she might bring Tina something. Her appearance was quite out of the ordinary: not the island type. She was as far from their standard of slim blond athletic good looks as her own elongated ungainliness.

As Tina placed her order she noted the plastic placard pinned to that capacious uniformed bosom—Maria.

"Can you be the Maria who used to work for the Hemmingway's?"

"Oh, yes," was the cheerful reply in a voice marked only by the faintest of accents. "I worked there but here I work now for the summer. I think I will like the job much better. More people in and out, you see. I like to be in a place which is busy. There is, the word is, yes, more opportunity." And she deftly filled a cup of coffee for Tina and brought it to her, efficiently producing the cream pitcher and two packets of sugar, and then returned to the end of the counter and her dish towel and glasses. Tina was stunned. Somehow, the varying remarks she had heard had not prepared her for *this* Maria, nor to find her happily established with a job on the island for the rest of the summer. It was not at all what Lilly had led her to expect. No wonder Tony Corbin had remembered her. Radiant Maria was really quite unforgettable.

A bell tinkled over the shop door and three boys entered heading for the counter. In the mirror Tina saw that one of them was Goddard, looking somewhat self-conscious but not at all surprised to see Maria as he followed the others down to the far end of the counter. Indeed, he seemed far more startled to see Tina when she interrupted their discussion to pay her check and depart.

Tina decided that she no longer felt in the mood for

shopping, and she mounted her bicycle and pedaled off in the direction of Mallard Cottage.

As Lilly had surmised, the girls seemed to bear her no particular animosity. They had just finished breakfast when she returned home and were ready to ride down to the beach club for the day. Tina accompanied them. She was considering reopening last night's conversation, for she was quite concerned that the girls had been so casual about smoking marijuana, but hesitated. This was clearly something Lilly should handle, even if she did not appear disposed to do so. Perhaps it was quietly accepted in island society, as long as scandal was avoided. Anyway, she did not want to lose the girls' friendship, to be relegated to the status of the despised Maria—a snoop.

The girls dove into the water, happily splashing one another. Each, from years of lessons, was an excellent swimmer and Tina deliberately put aside her concern, determined to let none of her speculations disturb this lazy day in the sun.

Lunch was something they signed for and ate in their swimsuits while sitting on the beach club deck under a striped umbrella. Their chairs were set out for them by a beach boy; the attendant at the ladies' pavillion furnished them with towels and took charge of their wet suits when they had changed out of them. Indeed, once she had made her decision to relax, the whole morning passed so pleasantly that by noon Tina felt far more charitable toward the island and its summer colonists than she had ever dreamed she could. Several of the Hemmingways' and Mallards' old friends had nodded greetings as she stood on line with her tray, and then sat with the girls in the shade, consuming the so easily obtained lunch and iced tea.

The water had been invigorating and the sun had put warm color into her usually pallid complexion, adding sparkle to her gray eyes. The spray seemed even to have helped her hair, whipping it into curling tendrils about her forehead, and into greater fullness all about her head: a flattering change from the skewered knot that her tightly wound hair usually looked like.

Later, as she dressed for dinner, Tina was conscious that the single day of vacation had been infinitely beneficial to her appearance. She was beginning to look almost as if she belonged here, rather than in the hot city apartment to which her mother would just be returning from work.

Mary Mallard sold dresses—or collection clothes to be more precise—at Bergdorf's, the milieu she preferred, even if at one remove. She had her ladies, her select clientele, whom she assisted with the assemblage of their wardrobes, and with many of whom, she could flatter herself, she was on a first-name basis. Tina had often had concrete reason to be grateful for her choice of work, since somehow her mother managed to keep Tina's lanky figure adequately attired at reasonable prices via store discounts and "channels," although Tina adamantly resisted any maternal attempts to clothe her in something "smart."

As she was often reminded by her mother, the Mallard family would be under no further obligation to Tina once she was twenty-one. She would soon be on her own, her education not quite completed, with only three-quarters of a degree in the unremunerative field of Mexican archaeology to her name. Proper attire and poise would help. She would have to find a job ultimately while she finished her last year at school and, after putting herself through, see whether there was any chance of employment in a museum, at a college, somewhere where she could use her knowledge while managing to live on a tiny salary. It did seem unfair, at times, that so much money was being squandered on lessons for her cousins with no objective in mind but to fit them for a life of total leisure.

Tina put aside these thoughts to go down to dinner, wondering as she went if Lilly, who seemed to know so much of what went on with the expenditure of so little effort, had as yet been informed of the present whereabouts of the enigmatic Maria.

Chapter 6

Crossing the hall toward the dining room Tina stopped abruptly. Her name had been called. Lilly was entertaining a few friends over drinks before dinner at the club. In past years, Tina might have been the recipient of an offhand introduction as she passed through a large group of guests, but now Lilly was actually calling her into the living room to join them.

Tina swallowed hard. This, then, was it, the opportunity of which she had been instructed, so optimistically by her mother, to avail herself. As firmly as she had resolved not to seek such occasions, there was no way to avoid this one without outright rudeness. She had one half-second in which to prepare herself to project maturity, interest, poise; all qualities which she would have to improvise. Tina bared her teeth in a fixed smile and, involuntarily, stooped a bit as she entered the room and crossed with barely restrained rapidity to the lounge opposite the door upon which Lilly reclined. For an instant Tina towered over her as the two gentlemen in the group rose to their feet. She was presented to Diane and Cap Wigmore, an older couple, the bridge champions of the island. She tried to modulate her ferocious smile as she sank gratefully into the vacant space beside the older woman. She could hardly focus on the individuals turned toward her as introductions were made. Gradually, her ability to connect names with faces returned. Tina found herself seated adjacent to Suki McCormick, another old friend of Lilly's, whom she could remember encountering on previous visits. The recollection did not appear to be mutual. On the other side of the coffee table sat a slender, tanned blonde, Sally Mallard, a relation who had come up from Texas for the summer and rented a nearby cottage for her extensive juvenile brood so as to reforge bonds with the eastern wing of the family. As Cap Wigmore resumed his seat, Tina felt herself encircled. Lilly remained languidly in her chair, somewhat removed from the group around the coffee table. The light of the lamp behind her shone on her fair hair and browned shoulders, set off by the white-crepe haltered pajamas which sheathed her lithe form and fell in silky folds to the foot of the chaise. Still on his feet next to her was the tall man who had been lounging on the hassock drawn up to the foot of Lilly's seat when Tina entered.

"Tina, you know Charles, don't you?" Lilly asked, offhandedly. When Tina failed to utter the requisite acknowledgment, Lilly continued smoothly, "I thought surely you'd met. This is Charles Corbin."

She inclined her shining head to look up at him.

"Fix Tina a drink, won't you, Charles?"

As he moved to the bar in the corner of the room, Tina felt oppressed by the thickening silence until Suki McCormick, raising a slim, tanned arm, jingling with bracelets, to smooth her hair, inquired with an air of painstaking exposition, "You're really Lilly's stepdaughter, aren't you, Tina? You see, Sally's forgotten just exactly how you fit in."

Tina glanced at Suki's bland face, the mask of a wax

doll held too near the fire for a fraction of a second, so that the peripheral contours had melted, bubbled, and settled unattractively between neck and chin. She added, mentally, and you want to make sure that we all remember my place, don't you. With effort, she responded in a small voice, "Yes, that's true. I live in New York City with my mother who was married to Goddard Mallard before he married Lilly."

Sally Mallard picked up the scent. "Oh, I see. And who was she? Before they married."

Before Tina could frame a reply, Suki supplied helpfully, "Nobody—I mean nobody you'd know, dear. A girl he married while he was at Yale."

Tina glanced quickly at Lilly, but her head was turned away in the direction of the bar. She found herself retorting in a strained voice, "Not quite nobody. Her name is Mary Mallard and she is my mother."

"Excuse me," Suki offered, her eyebrows raised, "I'd no idea of offending you."

At that moment, mercifully, Charles Corbin called across the bar, "Tina, I hate to admit it, but I'm not that good as a bartender after all. I can't find an opener anywhere." Grateful for rescue, Tina stumbled from her corner of the couch and passed into the half shadow behind Lilly's chair where Charles stood at the bar as Lilly turned her attention to her guests and asked Diane Wigmore a question. Tina found herself gazing up at Charles Corbin, a long way up. He was even taller than she had supposed. As his large hands fiddled with the various silver implements adorning the top of the bar while he made a show of conducting an unsuccessful search, she saw that he was handsomer than any man this large had a right to be. His blond hair was cut short, crisp; his eyes were light and seemed to be lazily laughing at his own awkwardness. He gave her a quick look and in an undertone remarked casually, "You can't take seriously anything Suki blurts out when she's drinking, you know."

Tina had regained her composure and managed an only slightly tremulous smile. "I don't take it seriously. After all, she says what she's thinking—or, what passes for thinking."

He laughed.

"You did come to my rescue deliberately, didn't you?" Tina said, reaching for the bottle opener lying half under the lid of the ice bucket where Charles had ineffectively hidden it. She held it out to him, a warm smile on her lips.

Charles shrugged. "Lilly told me you were shy, but she didn't mention that you were sharp, too."

Tina blushed as he deftly mixed her a gin and tonic. Curiosity impelled her to ask, "I suppose you must be related to Tony Corbin?"

"He's my kid brother. If you've met Tony, you've met the white hope of our family. He's the fair-haired boy. Really, we're very proud of him—he's quite a serious sailor."

"Yes, I've heard," said Tina. "He also told me that he's at Dartmouth and planning to go to medical school."

Charles laughed again good-humoredly. "If he's told you all about those plans you must know my little brother pretty well."

"Oh, no. We met just once, quite briefly."

Charles handed her the drink and turned to escort her back to the lighted part of the room. Lilly's other guests appeared to be engrossed in the conversation they had resumed.

Diane Wigmore was patting into place her gray streaked hair which curled, like the rim of a soup bowl, around her neck from ear to ear. Despite her coiffure, and the plunging décolletage of her orange ruffled blouse, she struck Tina as masculine in contrast to Cap, her husband. He must have been in his sixties yet managed to convey an air of cherubic youth, especially in this light which made it hard to distinguish the liver spots from the freckles that adorned his pudgy face. Cap beamed jovially at the circle of females surrounding him as he listened with sympathy to Sally Mallard's tale of the tribulations she'd encountered in the division of property necessitated by her pending divorce from her husband, a personage already so decisively dismissed from her life that not even his surname was recalled.

Suki's attention was wandering: she inspected her bracelets, her manicure; then adjusted the folds of her elaborate patchwork evening skirt. Cap, patting Sally's hand under Diane's equable gaze, was saying coaxingly, "Now that's the very reason you did the right thing in coming back to the island where we all know you, where you belong. Another few weeks and all these annoyances will be behind you." He seemed to Tina to have the appropriate pastoral bearing; the original Wigmore to settle on the island as a summer haven had been a minister, first minister of the summer chapel. Subsequent generations of Wigmores had somehow managed to remain aloof from the specific entanglements of the vocation, but whether it was genetic or environmental, Cap had obviously fallen heir to the manner.

Suki changed the subject abruptly. "Even the island isn't what it was when I was growing up," she said plaintively. "Your mother would be absolutely appalled at the change, Lilly. Standards have definitely fallen. Every cottage used to have its own staff. We used to be able to entertain properly. How many of us still have our own gardeners, chauffeurs, even housekeepers now? I know that I have to scrape by with a daily. My God, that's why we're always eating over at the club." She glanced over at Lilly, to see if she had been sympathizing with her complaints, but Lilly's expression failed to offer the commiseration which her best friend expected. Smiling sweetly, Suki added, "I don't mean you, of course, Lilly. But then, the rest of us *have* to be good with money. We don't have Findlay's wealth at our disposal. And it seems that even you have had to face the unpleasant realities. Dismissing that girl who was looking after the children must be a saving." Again Lilly failed to react to the implantation of this shaft. Suki went on: "When one has to think of managing, it takes half the joy out of vacation. And the result is that the children are running wild, positively taking over the island. I can't get a tennis court when I want one; I have to be careful not to even look in the dunes if I go for a swim in the afternoon, and as for the golf course, I'm sure it's used more at night than in the day. Of course, Lilly, you've been very clever," here Suki shot a glance at Tina, "but not everyone has the resources you have." Suki herself was childless and had frequently been heard to congratulate herself on her good fortune in having avoided this dreary encumbrance. "I just wish that others, who shall be nameless, were a bit more considerate of their neighbors and took the trouble to keep their offspring under control."

Lilly had stiffened during the course of this tirade by her dear friend. But they were old friends and Lilly knew that more lay behind this cri de coeur than had yet been disclosed. They were all quite used to Suki's bemoaning the need to practice economy; they had heard it for years without perceiving any resultant change in her style of living. Something in particular was on Suki's mind; there must be more to come. Lilly finally inquired, "And what exactly has set you off on this tangent tonight, Suki? Do tell us, I'm sure you're dying to."

Suki needed no further urging. "Drinking is one thing, and for that matter so is sex. I mean, we all grew up here, at one time or another." She looked over at the Wigmores, but they were listening avidly and did not seem to have taken offense. Sally Mallard was interested but complacent about Suki's imminent disclosures. "But drug orgies seem to me to be quite another matter. There are some parents on the island who are willfully blind to what's going on, but I, for one, think that steps should be taken."

Cap Wigmore, quite unshaken by the general tenor of Suki's revelation, sought more details. "Oh, come on Suki. What do you mean, drug orgies?"

As they awaited her reply, the members of her rapt audience automatically reached for their drinks and took a preparatory swallow. Suki paused to command their full attention.

"Well, I just happened to drive down to the beach club last Tuesday, after closing time. I thought I might have left a bracelet in my locker by mistake," she explained. "There were a dozen mattresses from the chaise longues piled on the sand, and I don't know how many kids were lying there, smoking pot, or worse. Of course, it was dark and I couldn't be absolutely certain who was there, but I know that if I had a teenage daughter on the island this summer, I'd be locking her in her room at night."

Diane Wigmore's disappointment was evident as she asked, "Then you don't actually know who was there?"

Suki looked put off. "They couldn't have been anyone but kids from the island, could they?"

"Oh, not necessarily, you know," Cap intervened pacifically. "It could have been some of the help, or even people who'd come over by boat."

Suki sniffed. "Oh, you can believe that if you want to."

Charles Corbin intervened for the first time. "I don't suppose the important point is exactly which kids they were, but where it's coming from and how it can be stopped."

Tina suddenly found herself speaking: "That is, if anyone around here considers it serious enough to risk the possible embarrassment of making an issue of it."

A shocked silence followed.

"But of course, Tina," admonished Lilly, "no one takes it lightly. We're all quite aware that it's against the law. I can't say that personally I can see any great harm in smoking marijuana on occasion, but hard drugs are quite a different matter. In either case, none of us wants to see a public scandal. The last thing we can do is to call in the authorities, so I must say, I can't see what steps we can take. I've spoken to my girls, and I imagine that the other parents will just have to do the same. I can't ruin the entire summer over a fad that's bound to blow over, anyway."

Suki rallied to Lilly's aid. "Of course, no one could criticize you, dear. You're just luckier than most in not having to pay someone to watch over your children." Resting her eyes on Tina's hot face, she added, "I do hope that your confidence isn't misplaced. It's so hard to find people who are able to give satisfaction, isn't it?"

Without waiting for Lilly's reply, Tina went over to the bar and replaced her glass. To Charles, who had risen to follow her, she said in a small voice, "Do you know, I don't really think I want this, after all. But thank you." Walking with quick steps to Lilly's side, Tina stopped and said quietly, "I'd better be going in to dinner. The children will be down now. You'll excuse me, I know."

Lilly appeared quite unperturbed. "How thoughtful. Of course, run along."

Chapter 7

Tina didn't think that she could bear any further attempts at mingling in the society of those who seemed so firmly committed to putting her in her place. She vowed again that she'd restrict herself to fulfilling the requests made of her so far as the children were concerned, and otherwise remain aloof. A few days passed peacefully enough, and she remained firm in her resolve, encountering neither Tony Corbin nor his attractive brother Charles in this interim. Lilly was out almost constantly and Tina started to feel as if she were in charge of the household. In fact, Mrs. Chambers began to ask her about plans for marketing, for meals and even the children's dinner guests.

Her relationship with Mimsi, Brooke, and Leigh had settled back into an old pattern—they patronized her faintly but were more grateful than not to have her to consult with about what clothes to wear, friends to visit, and matches to play. Goddard was out as much as his mother—sailing, Tina assumed, or else sitting at the feet of Tony Corbin, the Yacht Club guru. Finny occasionally haunted her footsteps for a few hours but seemed happy enough on Tuesdays and Thursdays, his riding days, and only slightly rebellious on the days she managed to get him on the day-camp bus for his swimming, tennis, and other lessons in competitive sports. Of course, sometimes she didn't catch him, but since he then remained out of her way for most the day, she assumed he was happy.

She and the girls, and Finny sometimes, frequented the Kraut's, where the younger crowd usually met after dinner for ice cream, or stopped in for a midafternoon snack on cloudy days. Maria, she saw, was as efficient as she had been at their first encounter. Interestingly, the girls had fallen into a pattern of merely giving her their orders and thanking her for service. To them she had metamorphosized from Maria into "waitress" by donning a uniform. Had she not been aware of the general tendency of her relations to treat those who served them as depersonalized entities, Tina would have thought this behavior remarkable; but as it was, she assumed it was all of a piece with the standards of conduct that Lilly had instilled in them: charming to equals and oblivious of inferiors—with no need to adopt a mode of behavior to those superior to themselves, the question never having arisen. For each girl the classification was set by her mother's standards and hers had been set by her mother's, based on the Social Register in part, with certain genealogies as bibliographic references and occasional footnotes with asterisks for a few, very few, names closely connected with new money, if the name was not too inappropriate and the money was deemed to be both clean and sizable.

Maria appeared to have collected quite a following amongst the younger set which customarily hung out in the coffee shop, Tina noticed. Too bad, she thought, that there are so few targets of a more appropriate age for her undoubted charms. But Tina had revised her estimate when, bicycling home with the girls from a beach party late one night, she passed a couple stumbling down a byway from the shore toward a car parked by the side of the road. One was undeniably Maria, and the other tall enough at least to be Tony Corbin.

Afterward she found her thoughts turning frequently, sometimes with envy, toward Maria. It must be enjoyable to be on one's own, with no ill-defined position to maintain, to be an absolute stranger in a community, free to behave exactly as one wanted. But, as Tina reminded herself savagely, in order to take advantage of such liberty it would help to be overtly attractive, like Maria, and not an awkward introvert. In truth, Tina sometimes found that she was chafing at the role to which she had consigned herself. Her consolation, the thought that at least she was needed, did not always suffice. Despite her resolve to remain independent, she found herself daily more deeply engaged with the problems and concerns of her family. Feelings of responsibility to them were engendered in her not only by confidences with which they had entrusted her, but also by Lilly's virtual abdication. As the extent of Tina's duties enlarged, there also arose an ever-increasing feeling of obligation. Why she should have been put in this position Tina hardly understood. She could only explain it by the fact that Lilly would undoubtedly take the path of greatest convenience, and was satisfied that Tina would be loyal, on family grounds, and unobtrusive but grateful, on personal ones. Tina assured herself once more that she could be content to live vicariously, and in any event, it was temporary.

One rainy Wednesday when she was waiting at the coffee shop for the girls to join her, Maria engaged her in conversation.

"So, then, how is everything at Mallard Cottage?" Maria asked with an interest which struck Tina as unusual in its intensity. "Mrs. Hemmingway, she does not miss me with you there, I suppose. As long as there is someone there to do the work she is content, yes? And is the master coming home soon?"

Tina thought: so this is the inquisitive side of Maria which got under the girls' skins. I suppose her curiosity is only natural, and I don't really blame her if she's bitter toward Lilly. It seemed to her that there had been a misunderstanding and that Lilly had behaved very high-handedly indeed. And then, Tina had never approved of the lofty manner which the girls had seen fit to adopt toward Maria. She determined to be friendly and replied as easily as she could, "Yes, everyone is well, thank you. But we don't really expect Mr. Hemmingway to be here this summer; I believe his travels will keep him in Africa for some time to come."

"So," Maria received this information thoughtfully, with what seemed to be a touch of disappointment.

Tina expected that their interchange was concluded, but Maria had a new topic in mind. First, however, she turned to the mirrored wall in back of her where she could compare her reflection with Tina's. Maria's plump, rosy attractions had been enhanced since her arrival at the restaurant by a more sophisticated coiffure and the addition of bright lip and eye color. In her orange sateen uniform, she made an eye-stopping picture. Next to her, Tina faded into the dimness of the room. Her unruly hair had escaped its restraint and fell in tangles over her forehead. Her heavy eyebrows furnished the only punctuation to the long, monochrome oval of her face. A navy sweater provided concealment as well as warmth. Her light eyes peering out under the dark brows faltered as they observed the contrast between the two of them in the mirror. Apparently well satisfied that she appeared to advantage, Maria again confronted Tina over the marble-topped counter which separated them.

"You may be quite suited, but that was not the proper place for me, in any case," she confided. "It is much better for me here. I see everyone, I know everyone. I have opportunities and I make the most of them. A girl like me cannot be expected to bury herself in the house as a domestic, after all."

Tina was gratified at Maria's satisfaction with events. At least she was not being blamed, however unjustifiably, for Maria's having been fired. Maria seemed to be wanting some response, and Tina hastened to express agreement. "I'm sure you're right."

Then Maria went on: "I am young, I am good-looking. If I wanted to be a servant I could have stayed at home. No, no, one comes to America to make a success, perhaps to line one's pockets with the gold from the streets."

Tina could not help being amused by the contrast between the girl's words and the position of waitress in which she had apparently found fulfillment of her aspirations. She was, after all, quite a simple girl. Tina could not imagine why Maria should be interested in convincing her, of all people, that she had no regrets for the job from which she had been dismissed. "Then it's all worked out for the best," Tina concluded.

The door to the restaurant was pushed open and a gust of damp air rushed through the overheated room. Maria turned away from Tina, remarking, "Perhaps not yet; but I think it will."

As Maria took the orders of the two entrants who had seated themselves in a booth by the door, Tina looked after her thoughtfully. She couldn't help feeling that Maria's words had in some way been at odds with her meaning.

Tina was distracted by the arrival of Mimsi, Brooke, Leigh, and their crowd. She heard about their plans for the evening, gave permission for them to go off the island to the movies with some friends if the weather continued to be dreary, and agreed to their inviting some guests over after dinner the following day. There were some things about her routine that were pleasurable, and her comfortable relationship with the girls was one of them.

The peaceful interlude, however, was destined to come to an end. Encountering Lilly at breakfast on the subsequent morning she was surprised to be informed, "Tina, I'm worried about Goddard. He doesn't want to stay on the island for the rest of the summer. He says he's bored with sailing. He's written to a school friend, some boy named Anderson, and he proposes to visit him in Arizona until he goes back to school in the fall. What in the world's prompted this?"

"But perhaps he *is* bored, Lilly," Tina replied reasonably. "Fourteen can be such an awkward age." As can sixteen, eighteen, and twenty she continued silently to herself.

"Of course, I know he's an adolescent. But I don't treat him as a child. He has all the freedom he could want." True, Tina agreed, inwardly. "And Goddard can't actually mean that he's bored with his boat. Why he lives for the summers, just so he can sail. He's had his heart set on entering the big races since he was Finny's age. He didn't even want to go to St. Paul's because it's inland; he wanted to go to some other place at Newport just so he could keep on sailing all year round. And I thought he'd fallen into such a good relationship with the Corbin boy. It's so important for Goddard to have an older male whom he can look up to. He can't remember your own father, and Findlay never seemed to fill that role for Goddard. I thought that he was identifying so beautifully with Tony—almost as if he were an older brother."

"Perhaps, then, you should speak to Tony," Tina suggested. "He must see more of Goddard than any of us. Maybe he can explain it."

Lilly looked pleased. "That's what I was thinking myself. Would you, Tina? It will be easy for you to stop in at the Yacht Club during the day and snatch a few words with him, won't it? I'd do it myself, of course, but I had made plans for today. Actually, Charles is taking me to

the other end of the island to teach me skin-diving—or
is it called snorkeling? It's something I've always wanted
to pick up. I'd hate to put it off and if I'm to go I'll have
to have a lunch packed for us right away. Do take care
of it, Tina. I'm sure you can cope. Why it would be
ridiculous to send Goddard all the way to Arizona for
the rest of the summer. He'll be away at school all winter
as it is. And we haven't even met this boy's people—we
don't know any Andersons. It would be much better if
you arranged with Tony Corbin to keep Goddard happy,
here."

Naturally, Lilly wouldn't want to spoil her plans
for a day alone with Charles Corbin although usually
they traveled with a group of old friends in atten-
dance so that their relationship had not seemed particularly significant. Tina, however, reproved herself
for her thoughts, acknowledging that she felt more
than a twinge of jealousy toward Lilly. She had already had two husbands, one of whom was still vital,
if only periodically present, and it did seem too bad if
she was on her way to annexing Charles, the most
personable, and Tina thought, the nicest man she'd
ever encountered. Their meetings, since Tina's disas-
trous introduction to Lilly's set, had been brief and
infrequent, confined to greetings as they passed each
other in the village and at the beach club, but he had
been unfailingly courteous to Tina and she had always felt that some degree of warm personal interest
in her emanated from him. Yes, Charles Corbin had
always been pleasant to her—but there was no possible reason, even if he suddenly lost interest in Lilly,
to suppose that he would transfer his attention to
Tina. It was ludicrous even to dream of competing
with Lilly for this attractive man who was, after all,
quite entitled to while away what seemed to be his
endless leisure in the pursuit of the most glamorous
of the many equally idle and temporarily unattached

sophisticates with whom the island was so well populated.

Well, she'd have to go to Tony on another missionary enterprise, this time on Goddard's behalf, even though, from her last brief encounter with him, she doubted that he would be willing to bestir himself in the slightest.

Having promised, Tina managed to loiter around the Yacht Club for a quarter of an hour at lunch time when, she thought, Tony would be finished with the morning's schedule of instruction. Goddard, she was relieved to note, was nowhere in evidence, although she saw several boys of his age leave the club and walk up the gangplank toward their bicycles on shore. She meandered over to where Tony was sitting crosslegged on the deck of the club untangling some lines. He looked up as her shadow blocked his light.

"Well, it's Tina Mallard. Here to sign up for sailing lessons?" he asked with a grin.

"No, thank you. I don't think there's anything I want to learn that you could teach me."

"Oh, really." Tony eyed her quizzically. "You do have quite a chip on your shoulder. I certainly rubbed you the wrong way the night of the dance. You take yourself much too seriously, you know." He glanced back at his knotted line.

"Please, I'm here at Lilly Hemmingway's request. I've no wish to have a discussion with you about *my* attitude. She's worried about Goddard. He says he's not interested in sailing any more and he wants to spend the rest of the summer off the island. Do you know why he should have lost interest in sailing so suddenly? Until now its been his main object in life."

Tony laughed up at her. "As a matter of fact, I could make a good guess. But, I thought I'd told you last time we talked—a good while ago wasn't it—that nursemaiding these kids was not part of my duties."

"But Goddard must be very unhappy. And we have no

59

idea what's come over him. Surely, if you have some idea, if you could tell me how to help him— You'd put yourself out that much?"

"You really don't have an inkling, do you?" Tony paused for a moment, reflecting. "You know, I like Goddard, I really do. He doesn't have any friends, but I get along with him all right. Just now I'd say he's going through a difficult stage. There'd be no point in telling Lilly, and I don't see how *you're* going to help, but I don't think he's at all bored with sailing. He's good and he's getting better, he's been winning quite a lot of the races we run in the Bullseye class. The cause and cure for his problem is right across the street." And Tony looked across the gangplank, into the sunny main street of the village.

Tina followed his gaze, bewildered, seeing only the awning-shaded façades of a few of the smart shops and the glinting plate-glass exterior of the coffee shop. "I still don't understand you. Must you be so oblique?"

Maddeningly, Tony began to half hum, half sing the opening bars of a vaguely familiar song. As Tina waited in perplexity, he vocalized the few concluding words which she simultaneously recalled ". . . and they called the wind, Mar-i-a . . ."

"Oh, but that's ridiculous. You don't mean that he's unhappy because he has a crush on Maria? Why, he's only fourteen, she must be at least my age."

"But there is a certain something about Maria. Hadn't you noticed," Tony replied mockingly.

"But she can't have given him the least encouragement. He's just a kid—I didn't think he even noticed girls. Why, he has as little as possible to do with his sister and cousins and their friends. It's absolutely ludicrous."

"Oh, do act your age, Tina. Boys of fourteen are well out of the sexual latency period. And this thing that's known as sexual attraction does not follow rigidly defined age categories. With Goddard and Maria it goes the same way as with Charles and your Aunt Lilly.

Tina was too startled to react to all the implications of his remark. "But poor Goddard. I don't know what anyone can do for him. He'd resent anything I said to him, I'm afraid."

"Well, yes, I think he might. You could suggest to Lilly that she raise his allowance substantially," Tony paused, "or, if that idea shocks you, better let him leave the island. He'll get over it."

This time Tina was truly perplexed. She watched as Tony bent forward again over the snarled lines and seemed to become reabsorbed in his work. Staring at his long sun-bleached hair Tina remained frozen while she sought to make some sense out of his remarks. Finally, with a shake of her head she requested, "I don't understand you. If you have something to say, why can't you speak plainly, instead of teasing me?" Tony whistled softly. "Well, since you ask, I simply mean that Goddard could get what he wanted, if he could pay for it. Since she went off your aunt's payroll, I'm sure Goddard has found that Maria's favors have been withheld from him although, I expect, they've been granted judiciously enough to others of his appreciative friends. Don't you know that the Kraut's is now the most popular spot in town for the kids, such as it is. Does it shock you? Would you like to call in the town constable?"

Tina flushed. "You can't mean it."

"Oh, yes. Maria is the island's latest recreational attraction. A multitude is grateful to your Aunt Lilly for converting it from a private sport to a public pastime."

Tina recoiled. "You are crude beyond belief."

Tony answered, "Rude, crude, and socially unacceptable—isn't that what the kids say?" He reflected a minute. "No, it's lewd, crude, . . . Well, that fits, too. So sorry if I've shaken you up." But he looked far more amused than sorry at her discomfiture.

"But Maria doesn't look at all that sort of girl. And

you're implying, somehow, that Lilly knew . . . about her, when she worked for us."

"Oh, yes. A wholesome girl, with a hearty natural appetite. No other kind need apply. It's an old family tradition—in old families, that is. My, you have a lot to learn, Tina." But Tina had turned on her heel and was hurrying, blindly, down the gangplank. Tony Corbin had been deliberately teasing her, had intended to embarrass her, but she was sure that his account of Goddard's problems was in some part true. In fact, what she had liked least about the entire interview was that he seemed so absolutely certain of his information. Could he be so sure without first-hand knowledge? That rankled quite as much as the deliberate exposure of her naïveté to his amused gaze.

Chapter 8

Tina's perplexity increased as the afternoon wore on. The girls were playing in tennis matches and so she was free, but her thoughts that afternoon on the beach were interspersed with twinges of shame as she caught herself looking wonderingly at each adolescent boy who passed. She was thankful that Goddard was not there, so that she could avoid talking with him for the present, and she had no idea of what she should reveal of Tony's supposed information to Lilly, who would surely want to know, sooner or later, the gist of her interview.

She was one of the last to leave as the club closed for the afternoon. The locker room attendants were sweeping accumulations of sand out of the carpeted aisles onto the boardwalk through which it cascaded to the dunes below, and the restaurant attendants were folding umbrellas and up-ending chairs upon tables. But her passage down the steps was barred by Tony Corbin, lounging at the bottom of the short flight down to the parking lot; he was leaning casually against the bike rack which held her only means of transportation.

She looked about her helplessly—at the sky, at the blue

water sparkling behind the dunes. Then, there being no other choice, she descended the flight of steps.

"I've been waiting for you for over ten minutes," he said to her surprise.

"Well, I certainly didn't expect you, and I can't honestly say that I'm sorry to have kept you waiting."

"I thought we could talk some more. I didn't think I'd get to you so badly. Why did you run away in a panic? Say, you're really hung up on sex, aren't you?"

Tina's cheeks flamed. "Look, we are not going to discuss *me*. In fact, I can't think of anything at all that I want to discuss any further with you."

"You know, I find you rather fascinating, Tina. You're a virgin, aren't you? I didn't believe there were any left —at your age," he stated coolly.

"How dare you? I'm not listening to you. Let me get my bike or I'll hit you," she raged between clenched teeth.

"You've got the reach, but somehow I don't think you'd pack much of a wallop. I'll take my chances," he concluded.

"Tony Corbin, I hate you. I thoroughly abominate you and detest you," Tina shouted at him.

"Fine. I knew you'd find something you wanted to say to me. Now can we talk about it?" he answered, quite calmly.

"Where?" Tina spluttered. "Over a Coke at the Blue Danube, I suppose? You have enough nerve for anything, I'm sure."

"Why not?" Tony grinned. "Are you offering to treat? Whoops— I guess I should have ducked first," he said, as he grabbed her flailing fists in one hand. "Now simmer down. Really, I came over to make amends and see if I couldn't talk some sense to you. I *can* be quite sensible, you know, and it seems to me that Lilly Hemmingway has dumped quite a mess of worms in your lap."

Tina relaxed a little in his grasp, but looked into his eyes suspiciously. "I'm not sure it's safe to walk anywhere with you, particularly not on the dunes at nightfall."

"Aren't you big enough to defend yourself? No, I take it back. Don't hit me again, lady," he mocked. "Look, Tina, don't be so wary. I'm on my best behavior. Let's take a walk." And, still holding her by one wrist, Tony began to cross the parking lot toward the empty dunes which rose up in back of the club beach. Reluctantly, Tina fell into step beside him. When they reached the dunes, Tony sat and half pulled her down beside him, where they remained for a few moments watching the waves tumbling toward them.

Still irate, Tina broke the silence between them. "All right. I've taken a walk. We're alone. Now what sensible things do you have to discuss with me?"

Tony looked at her ruefully. "I meant what I said back there. I never dreamed you'd get so worked up over this. I mean, you take sex too seriously. You must be the first twenty-year-old virgin on the island in fifty years. Where have you been living all this time?"

"Not at one of your exclusive boarding schools, where the instruction appears to be more broadening. I live at home, with my mother."

"But don't you go out with men? No, I see. You study Mexican artifacts, day and night. Look, Tina, you're missing the boat. It's not as if you were ugly or deformed. You'd be quite passable-looking if you'd only forget to be self-conscious about your height. Why don't you loosen up, let your hair down, wear some makeup and some more attractive clothes. Why, I'll bet you could be a model if you fixed yourself up."

Tina looked at him with loathing. "You sound like my mother. But not every tall, plain girl is a model in chrysalis. There's no need to try to flatter me, if that's what you think you're doing. What exactly did you bring me up here for? I thought we were going to talk about Goddard."

"That was one subject I mentioned. But, I think I'd rather talk about you first. Why don't we get better acquainted? I'm at loose ends this summer and so are you —at any rate when you aren't riding herd on the kids for Lilly. Why don't you relax and enjoy yourself? There are still several weeks of vacation left. You could have a lot more fun than you're having now."

"And I suppose you're quite willing to show me how to relax and have fun. Why don't you just go home and ask your mother to raise *your* allowance?"

He threw his head back and laughed. "Touché. I don't know why I keep trying. I guess it's because you sure are different; it must be my collector's instinct. Your virtue has the virtue of rarity."

Tina looked at him, and crude as he was she had to admit that he was not unattractive physically. Not her ideal, of course, but tall and tanned and even good-looking in an unobtrusive sort of way. His unexpected bluntness fascinated as it repelled her.

"You really mean you want to have sexual intercourse with me, as a sort of favor to me, don't you?"

He replied, without hesitating, "It *would* be a good way to get to know each other. You can't deny that."

"Well, when I want to get to know you better, I'll let you know," said Tina, attempting to rise to her feet.

"You really are the strangest girl," Tony said, shaking his head as if her response had been unaccountable. "Well, there's nearly a month of summer left. I can be patient." He too rose, and Tina found that she was looking into his eyes as he stood close to her. She was strangely unable to summon her volition for flight; her mind told her to run, but her legs refused to answer. Tony leaned forward to close the gap of a few inches which had briefly separated them, and holding her lightly by the shoulders, kissed her softly, and then let her go. Taking her hand, he began to walk with her back to the steps of the beach club. "You see, I feel that I know you better already. I'll come by in my car at about ten."

Tina made no answer but, suddenly darting free, raced for her bicycle and started pedaling toward Mallard Cottage.

Chapter 9

Tony Corbin did stroll into Mallard Cottage after ten that evening. After a desultory search of the downstairs precincts of the cottage in which he deliberately avoided the sounds of hilarity issuing from the garden room at the side of the house he finally found Tina in the pantry.

The sight of him looming over her as she bent to fill several glasses from a gallon-size Coke bottle had a paralyzing effect on Tina. Tony quickly stepped forward and removed the Coke bottle from her hands. "You're spilling over. Watch it," he said. "My car's outside."

"I can't go. I never said I would go with you. I don't want to go. Anyway, I have to stay here; the girls have a gang in and they're all in the sun room."

"Where's Lilly? What about the staff?" he asked impatiently.

"She's not back, at least I don't think so. And Mrs. Chambers and the maid aren't working at this hour."

"But you are! Are you getting paid for this, or is it strictly voluntary?" he inquired sarcastically.

"No, of course I'm not being paid. I'm a Mallard, and

I'm here as a family guest, don't you see?" Tina was not entirely convinced that *she* did. "But I am responsible. I couldn't possibly leave a group like this alone in the house . . . even if I wanted to." Tina was quite sure in her own mind that she had no desire to take a ride with Tony, under the conditions and with the aims which had been laid down in their conversation that afternoon. At least she was almost sure, so why had she been so relieved when the decision had been taken out of her hands? "Won't you stay and have a coke?" she asked politely. "I'll just take these glasses into the sun room."

"Here, give me that," Tony said curtly, relieving her of the laden tray. "Just make sure to hold the doors." As she held the swinging door open, he preceded her out of the pantry and started across the width of the house. Tina followed in his footsteps.

The seven girls and three boys in the garden room looked up from their preoccupations when Tony Corbin entered the room. Standing in the entry Tina watched the blond heads follow his progress across the room like a stroboscopic exposure of sunflowers in a meadow.

"Drinks are served," he announced. "Dave, Bryan, come here and hand these around." Turning back to Tina, he enquired sweetly, "Back to the pantry for us? Or are you allowed to entertain callers in the living room, Miss Mallard?" Tina flushed crimson, observing the meaningful exchange of glances between her cousins Brooke and Leigh at this pronouncement by the unexpected visitor, and led the way into the front sitting room.

"For heaven's sake," she adjured him, "can't you restrain yourself from embarrassing me? What do you think they're going to say amongst themselves, and to Lilly?"

"I don't much care. Why should you? What sort of a summer vacation have you let yourself in for anyway?

Permanent unpaid governess, always on duty? Aren't you supposed to have any life of your own? You're being taken advantage of and you must know it."

"I don't understand why that should be any of your business," she told him.

"Oh, it's none of my business," Tony agreed. "I just wondered why you make yourself a doormat for the rest of them to walk on. I guess I've never run across anyone quite like you before, and I'm kind of curious."

"I don't know why I should have to satisfy your apparent insatiable curiosity, but if you must know, I like to help out. I prefer to feel that I'm needed here."

Tony looked at her searchingly, until her defiant gaze fell. "It sounds like a rather desperate rationalization to me."

"Now look," Tina said, "it would be silly of me to pretend that they really think of me as part of the family. I used to hope they would. But lately I'm not so sure I'd even want to be. If I'm being taken advantage of, and it doesn't bother me, why should it bother you? I like being useful."

"Useful or used?" he snapped.

She laughed. "I thought that using people was supposed to be the way of the world. I'm just adapting to it."

"Well, it may be the way of the world, but you don't have to roll over and beg for more. Somehow, you don't sound so intelligent tonight."

"Oh, I don't want to listen to you any more. I won't listen to you. Go away."

"Now who's unbelievably rude? But I'm going. I'll see you around," and the screen door slammed behind him as he left.

Returning to the party, Tina tried to appear unaware of the quizzical glances directed at her, although there was something gratifying in the realization that for the first time the girls were actually looking at her as a person. And while Tina shrank from what she judged to be the speculation in those glances, there was an immeasurable increase in her self-esteem from the simple fact that she had, for once, provoked *their* curiosity.

Chapter 10

The days passed lazily. Tina had quailed before the prospect of making a full revelation to Lilly of what Goddard's problem was, as expounded by Tony Corbin. She was still reluctant to place full credence in his information and there was no other basis for bringing Maria into the conversation. She did tell Lilly that Tony had attributed Goddard's changed attitude to a crush on a girl, which Lilly seemed to accept readily enough. "No need to worry about that, at his age," she said. "He'll be over it in a few days." Lilly had flatly refused to endorse Goddard's proposed trip to Arizona and, as far as Tina could observe, her half-brother continued to be moody but not crushed. His days were spent out on his boat, as before. Nothing appeared to have changed there.

But the attitude of her female relatives to her had been markedly transformed. The girls had suddenly subjected her to a concerted scrutiny and, almost like older sisters, had attempted to take her in hand. Tina knew well enough that she must appear like a great shaggy Irish wolfhound in a compound of sleekly groomed toy spaniels. She was only surprised that they hadn't taken one look, and abandoned the attempt. But, instead they were endearingly persistent.

"Tina, let me do your eyebrows," Mimsi had offered. "That nature's-child look is totally passé. Compare your eyes with mine. You see, the trick is to have thin arches! It'll change you completely; open up your face. You won't know yourself." Then the twins gave her the benefit of their advice: "I guess with your kind of hair you can't just part it in the middle and let it hang. But, for goodness' sake take all those bobby pins out. We'll give you a haircut ourselves. Then you won't have to keep it all pinned back."

Tina was amused. "Why all this sudden concern about my appearance. Are you afraid that I don't do you credit?"

"Well," Brooke blurted out, "we never thought you cared what you looked like. We didn't think you were interested in men. But if you want to get Tony Corbin, then we're going to have to shape you up. I mean, he won't pay any attention to us; he says we're too young, and *we're* absolutely gorgeous. So, if you want him you're going to have to redecorate a little and we'd be glad to help."

"Get Tony Corbin?" Tina said. "You're talking nonsense. He's totally rude and conceited beyond belief. Why, I've been doing my best to avoid him."

"Exactly!" chimed Leigh, triumphantly, quite satisfied with this as an expression of interest on Tina's part. "And you're so much older than we are that we're not a bit jealous. You need him much more than we do. So we'll help you."

Tina looked at the three perfect mannequin faces before her and was touched by their first instances of concern for her. Sensing her weakening, they went into full cry.

"You needn't worry, Tina, I know just how to cut your hair. I spent half of last term doing hairdos in the dorm."

"I think makeup too, don't you?" said Mimsi with a professional air. "Not much, but Tina really needs some color. We could put some shadows in back of her eyelids. And maybe a streak of pinky brown under each cheek-bone?"

"My goodness," Tina laughed, "you sound like three beauticians. Is this how you spend all your free time at school?"

Mimsi was shocked. "But Tina, it's so important. A girl's appearance means absolutely everything. Of course we work at it. Why at your age, I'd be ashamed to go around with an absolutely naked face. It's so uninteresting."

Tina was engaged by their obviously good-natured concern for her. "Well, all right, if you're such experts, I'll put myself in your hands. But *not* to help me get Tony Corbin as you so exquisitely expressed it. I don't want him."

The girls at least appeared to accept her disclaimer at face value and set themselves willingly to their task. Mimsi set to work applying an eyebrow tweezer with dexterity and at length, ignoring Tina's pained protests. Without allowing her any further voice in the matter, Brooke produced an alarming pair of shears which she wielded diligently under Leigh's instruction. Quantities of dark hair fell about them. Tina had long since passed into numb despair by the time the attack of the flying scissors ceased. But they refused to permit her to inspect the damage. Mimsi brought forth a veritable paint box, and, after selecting the colors for their palette, the three girls began to fingerpaint her face. Tina's usual choice of neutral lip gloss was laughed to scorn; they would not allow her caution to inhibit their self-expression. Green, blue, rose, brown, and silver were stroked, patted, and drawn upon her face. Tina's objection—"But I'll look like a clown"—was firmly ignored. The work went on; the two minutes normally expended by Tina in the task of preparing her face for public appearance had been surpassed ten times over when the girls came to a halt. They appeared well satisfied, but they were not yet finished. Mimsi said, "I can hardly believe it myself . . . and yet there's still something missing." A consultation followed, and the twins ran to their room and returned with a rosecolored scarf and a pair of hoop earrings enameled in a brilliant shade of pink. These ornaments were added and Tina was at last allowed to gaze into the mirror to see what they had wrought.

A vaguely familiar image confronted her in puzzled disbelief. The thick mop of brown curls had disappeared; only a waving umber cap remained to frame her face. Her light eyes appeared enormous, shaded in blues, brown, and silver. Her prominent nose had somehow receded to join up with the rest of her face. The rosy tones of her cheeks and the vivid pink of her lips were echoed by the earrings and scarf. The various components of her face had been drawn into an integral whole; she appeared to have been finely polished. Her face no longer swam in the glass like a hazy blur. Tina was taken aback; the countenance she saw in the glass was that of a stranger, sophisticated yet approachable.

"There. It's terrific," Brooke exulted.

"Frankly," Mimsi confessed, "we surprised ourselves. Tina, you're absolutely super! Look at what you've been wasting."

Tina was bemused. The creation she saw in the mirror was a work of art to which she bore only a remote connection. She was not sure she could appear in public with this glamorous façade, so alien to what she knew to be beneath it. But it was undeniable that she was exhilarated by the discovery that she could look so alluring. She had never imagined looking remotely like this. She studied her reflection in silence, which the girls took as adequate proof of gratification at the transformation which they had produced. They had no reservations to their delight. After an exchange of congratulations Leigh remarked, "I don't suppose you'll be able to do it yourself for a while, so we'll be glad to fix you up for next Saturday. Of course, there's still the problem of a dress to be considered." And she and her sister fell back a step to eye Tina appraisingly. Tina, while still transfixed by the novelty of her own face, had taken note of this observation. "What's this about Saturday? What have you three cooked up? This smacks of conspiracy."

"Oh, no," Mimsi said. "It's just that Saturday's the formal dance at the golf club to celebrate Cup Weekend. Everyone will be on the island and they'll all be going to the dance. I don't suppose anyone has asked you?" Tina's confirmation was accepted with a shrug. "But that's all right. We're going so Mummy will want you to go, too. Now, don't sit down on a chair on the edge of the floor, like a chaperone, and don't hang around with us kids all evening. You go over to the bar and get a drink and stand there looking interesting. That way you'll be noticed."

"Oh, I'm sure I'll be noticed," Tina laughed. "For one thing, I literally have nothing to wear. I'd be a standout all right." The girls' faces fell. They looked at each other questioningly. "Now don't even think it," Tina admonished. "I couldn't possibly borrow a long dress from any of you. It would come up to my knees. I think that you're trying to be very kind, and I do appreciate it, but believe me, I am not going to the dance on Saturday and I am not interested in any men on this island, especially not Tony Corbin."

Nonetheless, that Saturday evening, Tina found herself in the car accompanying the girls to the golf club. Her cousins and Mimsi had obviously found an occasion to talk to Lilly and Lilly had spoken to her. "But of course you must go to the dance, Tina. I depend on you. I never would have said that Mimsi, Brooke, and Leigh could form a table if I'd thought you wouldn't be keeping an eye on them. I'm going with a party of my own so I won't be able to keep track of them at all. So you must go. It's settled. Don't worry about what you'll wear. I'll take care of it." And Lilly had been true to her word.

A package was sent up from the village and when Tina and her assistants opened it, it revealed a simple emerald-green tube of material which, as Tina lifted it from its wrappings, seemed to go on forever. But when she tried it on she found that it covered her all the way down. The top was another story. Two shoestring straps of matching green satin held the dress up, and while Tina tugged gently to raise the dress up under her arms, the material kept falling disobligingly down to the level below the top of her bra. The girls, however, were enthusiastic.

"There, that's perfect. Mummy's got a terrific eye for clothes. Don't worry about the top. It'll be fine without a bra."

"Without a bra?" Tina protested. "I couldn't possibly go out with nothing on underneath."

"But you can't mean it. You'll spoil the dress. You're so flat-chested anyway, it won't matter. It'll never fit otherwise," they said, and Tina admitted the justice of their opinion when she experimented and found the dress adequately secure and much more attractive without the top of her white underwear protruding from its abbreviated décolletage. Having ventured that far, she became reckless, and voluntarily underwent a complete cosmetic overhaul on the night of the dance.

Gowned in unaccustomed splendor, transformed as far as scissors and paint could work their magic, Tina nevertheless was prey to trepidation when the car stopped under the red-and-white striped awning shielding the entry to the golf club. Yet she found herself with the others proceeding up the steps which led to a temporary ballroom area. With a last muffled instruction, "And don't let us catch you standing about with your arms folded across your chest," the twins followed by Mimsi fled across the as yet lightly populated dance floor, to the area in which their friends were congregated about a table graced by a punch bowl and lined with rows of glasses and bottles of Coca-Cola. Disobeying her detailed instructions, Tina immediately fled in the other direction, down a broad flight of stone steps which led into the nether regions of the clubhouse, and the ladies' locker room and adjacent lounge.

Fortunately, the lounge was unattended, and empty, so she sat down at the dressing table, wringing and rubbing her icy hands to try to get some warmth into them. Although she'd had time to school herself to the prospect of this dance, Tina was now terrified. She'd been to dances—mixers they'd called them—at high school, and then again, at college, where, having been driven by her mother's insistence, she'd stood frozen for what seemed like hours, looming in solitude over prospective partners who managed to remain oblivious of her existence. Before returning home she would spend the remainder of a decent interval either huddled down into a folding chair, in conversation with some girl with whom she was acquainted, or going on forays to the ladies' room which had had the advantage of keeping her feet from falling asleep. But at the mixers, at least, she was a misfit among misfits, for there were many others who came and left unattached, or, staying, populated the chairs along the side of the gymnasium floor, or thronged the ladies' room. Here she would be the only loner, and her unattached state and lack of acquaintance would proclaim her as an interloper. She had been able to endure this status at the Yacht Club junior dance because then she had obviously been a chaperone and only children had been present. Somehow she felt quite different about this dance. True, she looked far more attractive than ever before, but Tina did not delude herself that her appearance would win her admirers. Her cousins might have been able to cover her face with the proper veneer but, even if she held herself up straight, she would still be a gawky outsider condemned to wander the outskirts of this dance for the next three hours at least. Fortunately, before Tina could sink herself completely into a blue funk, some other women entered the ladies' lounge and, into their superficially smiling acknowledgment of her existence, Tina read curiosity as to her prolonged occupation of the dressing table. She was forced to rise, propel herself back up those granite steps, and enter the now crowded ballroom. The girls' instructions leaped to her mind like a lifeline and she crossed to the bar and in a cool voice requested the bartender to prepare for her the one drink whose name came to her out of the past. "Gin and tonic, please," she said and when an icy glass wrapped in a cocktail napkin was presented to her, she walked away a few paces and took a hesitant sip.

"I'm sorry that I'm too late to get you a drink," said a resonant male voice quite close to her but well over her head, and looking up to see who had spoken she found herself being addressed by Charles Corbin.

Trying quickly to swallow the unaccustomed drink, Tina choked, and to her mortification, Charles began patting her on her bare back in a paternal fashion.

"Excuse me, please," Tina mumbled in a small choked voice and turned away, but Charles gripped her arm firmly above the elbow.

"Here, I'll put that down for you. You don't really want it, do you?" he said. Without waiting for her response, he returned it to the bar and propelled Tina toward the dance floor.

"Are you going to dance with me?" she asked, awkwardly, without raising her eyes above the level of his chin, as he turned to face her. Putting his arm about her waist, he proceeded to demonstrate that that was, indeed, his intention. Gratefully, Tina relaxed in his arms, her tension and shyness momentarily, mercifully, departing as she realized that she was in fact dancing at the golf club with the most attractive man on the island or, maybe, in the world. Catching glimpses of her reflection in the mirror as they circled the room she was conscious of how well matched they were in size, for while he appeared to tower over all of the other women in the room and even to top the rest of the men by a few inches, the crown of her curly head came just to a level with his ear, so that when she looked up, finally, she was gazing almost directly into a pair of blue eyes looking down at her.

"Happier, now?" he asked. "You didn't seem quite to like your drink."

"Oh, yes, blissfully," she murmured before recovering herself. "Quite happy. You must dance quite well."

"Must I?" he laughed.

"That *is* a compliment." Tina explained, "What I meant was that since I'm quite awkward at dancing and we seem to be doing quite well, you must be extra good."

"To compensate, yes, I see," he replied. "But I hadn't noticed any awkwardness. It must be that we fit together so well, don't you think? It's a blessing to be able to put my arm about your shoulders and actually see your face when we talk, instead of groping down around my waist for my partner."

"I suppose that sometimes your height must have disadvantages for you too. I thought only tall girls had problems," Tina said.

"No. It's a constant affliction to me," he teased. "Can't sit in theater seats without sticking my legs into the aisle; can't enter a genuine colonial farmhouse converted to a summer cottage without cutting my head open on the lintel, can't find a pretty girl to dance with and, at the same time, whisper into her ear—until I found you."

Tina drew back and looked at him seriously. "Are you flirting with me?"

"Can't you tell?"

Tina wasn't sure that she could. These Corbins did seem to be the most unaccountable males. Somewhat suspiciously, she asked, "Where's Lilly?"

"Oh, I'm not with Lilly tonight. She formed her own table, and I wasn't invited. I'm here quite on my own, so you'll have to do me the favor of dancing with me whenever you're free—since we fit so well."

Tina smiled. She was grateful that he hadn't asked who her escort was, but she was still somewhat suspicious of his apparent interest in her. "Has Tony been talking about me to you?" she blurted out.

He looked at her with mild surprise. "I didn't know you were that well acquainted with Tony."

Tina was reassured. "Oh, no. We're not friends. Quite the opposite."

Charles gave her a look of mock relief. "For a moment there I was worried. It would never do to be trying to cut out my own brother, would it?"

Tina could hardly believe her ears. Charles sounded sincerely interested in her. He danced with her, brought her a Coke, and continued to draw her out as to her studies and her plans, and she began to bask in a sense of unwonted happiness.

Their easy colloquy was interrupted, however, by Tony, who appeared on the dance floor and came straight to the spot where Tina and his brother were standing. He said abruptly, " 'Lo Charles. Come and dance, Tina," as he drew her forward. She again found herself being steered about the dance floor, but in a far different fashion. "You look a lot better," Tony remarked, for openers.

"I suppose that's meant for a compliment," Tina replied coldly.

"Just a statement of fact. It's remarkable what a little

paint and a decent dress can do for a girl. You no longer look like Little Orphan Annie printed on a stretched-out piece of Silly Putty."

"You'll turn my head with such flattery!" Tina rejoined.

"Well, I was the one who told you to snap out of it. I'm glad my advice had such a good effect on you, and, of course, that's only the beginning. Just put yourself in my hands, and see how good you'll feel."

"Why, you conceited ape," Tina retorted. "If you think I'm trying to please you, you're way off the mark."

"Oh, ho. Someone else in your sights? Who could that be, I wonder? Not, not possibly, my handsome older brother?"

"Your brother may be handsome—"

"Oh, hadn't you noticed?" Tony interrupted.

"As I was saying, but more important, he is attentive and charming, qualities which you totally lack."

"And, so I gather, he's been dancing with you and you alone since he got here. And your head is turned. But you needn't fancy yourself as a femme fatale quite yet. Charles and Lilly have had a parting of ways and I imagine he's trying to annoy her."

"Meaning that he's just dancing with me to get back at Lilly! I don't believe you. Your *brother* isn't that kind of person." Tina felt herself color.

"Well, you seem to know him quite well, on brief acquaintance. Do tell me all about my brother," Tony suggested.

"For one thing, he dances with me a lot better than you do," Tina ventured.

"My, my. If you're not enjoying this dance, by all means let's step out on the terrace for a breath of cool air in the moonlight."

And he led her through the half-opened French doors onto the broad stone terrace which looked out over the first fairway. The cool air did have the effect of calming

Tina's annoyance, which she had to admit was less attributable to Tony's needling remarks, by now expected, and more to the fact that he had detached her from his brother's company. She was far from believing Tony's slurs against Charles, recalling that Tony seemed to have a penchant for putting the worst possible construction on everybody's behavior which she was no longer naïve enough to fully credit. Still, he was behaving almost like the dog in the manger about Charles. Could he possibly be jealous? Or had she indeed had her head turned? Could her surface improvements have really made such a difference? She was suddenly afraid that she might be making a fool of herself. Somewhat abashed, she turned to Tony on the darkened terrace. But before she could speak, he seized her by her bare shoulders and kissed her half-open lips.

Tina froze. As she was released, she asked him, seriously, "Did you kiss me just to make me angry again?"

Tony looked surprised. "It's not that I want to make you angry, Tina, it just seems to be the effect I have on you! I kissed you because I wanted to. It seems to me that you're rather in need of affection, whether or not you admit it."

"Do you realize how patronizing you are?"

"Am I?" He appeared to think this over. "I suppose so. But you've aroused novel sentiments in my manly bosom, my dear," he said with a mocking flourish, and continued, in declamatory style, "that's exactly what I propose being—your patron. I shall defend you from the slights put upon you and introduce you to the finer things of life which you've, inexplicably, missed out on."

"Hmph," Tina snorted, "for 'affection,' read 'seduction'! Let me tell you, I do not plan to allow you to round out your summer by seducing me."

"Oh, well," bantered Tony, "that's what you say now. And we both would have enjoyed it so much. Still, never say die, there are three weeks of vacation left. I swear you'll be a different girl by the time you leave this island."

"Maybe," Tina responded, "but not in the way you mean. Why should I want to enter into a relationship with you? You're always rude to me, sometimes I think deliberately."

"Well, it has had the result of bringing you out of that hard shell you've wrapped around yourself. Maybe just the least bit, but you're beginning to emerge. I'm interested in forwarding the process."

Tony's words recalled to Tina her own thoughts as she had approached Mallard Cottage. She had likened herself to a snail curled up in a shell. "But why in the world should I turn to you? Have you thought of that? What reason have you given me to like you, much less to fall in love with you?"

Tony recoiled, in mock horror. "Who said anything about love? That's all of a parcel with your other antiquated notions, my girl. I'm not a romantic, whatever my other failings, if any. I'm just proposing a closer acquaintanceship based on a certain amount of mutual attraction. And, for some unaccountable reason, I do like you."

"Well," Tina bristled, "since there seem to be no conventions or manners to restrain you from saying just what you please, I see no reason to restrain myself. Let me tell you, Tony Corbin, in no uncertain terms, I do not like you."

"That's intended to be final, isn't it?" Tony answered, not at all crushed by her attempt at a devastating retort. "But let's see if it's true." And before Tina could whirl away Tony seized her once more and held her to him. As Tina struggled, he raised her face to his and kissed her again, this time quite roughly. For a few moments Tina fought indignantly. But then, unaccountably she found herself participating. After what seemed a long time Tony released her and half laughing at her amazed look said, "Well, that did wonders for my bruised ego. I don't think you know yourself quite as well as you think you do." He turned and left her alone on the terrace.

"I hate you," Tina called after him softly, but even as she said it, she knew it was untrue.

Chapter 11

Recovering her shaky equilibrium, Tina smoothed her hair and dress, and returned to the noise and the crowd gathered on the dance floor. Recalling her charges, her eye sought them out. All three girls had partners and were engaged in a noisily gymnastic dance near the center of the floor.

Lilly approached her casually and with a smile thinly masking her icy tone of voice directed Tina to have the kindness to repair her makeup immediately. Tina quailed before her; unaccustomed to wearing lipstick, she hadn't given a thought to what she must look like. She fled, once again to the ladies' lounge, where she quickly made the necessary repairs. What must Lilly be thinking of her!

Tina wondered if she could possibly slip away by herself as she stood briefly looking out of the front door but she was once again claimed by Charles. And, to Tina's dismay, she saw that Lilly was quite near and her gaze was upon them. Unable to think coherently, she found herself once again dancing in the haven of Charles's arms.

"You weren't thinking of leaving?" Charles enquired. "I hope Tony didn't do anything to annoy you." Tina managed to shake her head. Charles continued, "You mustn't take too much notice of what he says. Sometimes I think he prides himself on his rudeness, but he calls it frankness. He's at that age, you know, when he's rebelling against all our 'stupid conventions,' as he calls them. And I'm afraid he lumps ordinary courtesy in with other, more serious social hypocrisies. Of course, he is right in some of his criticisms; youth always is right to a certain extent. Our world does have a tendency to overlook any sort of behavior as long as it's done with discretion, and that seems unpardonable to a kid like Tony so he goes in the opposite extreme."

Tina looked up at him in surprise. "It always seems to me that he's deliberately trying to provoke me. What I can't stand is his implying that I'm a naïve romantic while he's a realist."

Charles laughed. "You are just a little, aren't you? But delightfully so. Tony, on the other hand, is in the rather precarious position of having recently determined *not* to be naïve, and so he sees everything in a scrupulously pragmatic light. I'm afraid life is a little more complicated than that. But we're getting much too serious. I'm afraid you tend to have that effect on me, Tina," he said, but with the lightest of intonations. "Why don't you have dinner with me, and we'll see if we can't find some cheerful nonsense to talk about." Tina glanced involuntarily across at the "children's" table, but repressing the claims of duty, agreed hesitatingly. "All right. If you're sure . . . I mean you do want me to?" Charles lifted her chin with one hand and said casually, "I rarely do anything I don't want to do."

Tina joined him at a table which was already partly filled with his friends, mostly, she gathered, men in their late twenties and early thirties, who had come back to the island for the golf weekend, and their wives, or someone else's wives, and dates. Tina couldn't quite follow the rapid introductions which took place when she and Charles joined the table after filling their plates at the buffet. Still, no one seemed to stare at her enquiringly. Her neighbor on her left conversed with her, chiefly about his golf game, while Tina nodded and ate and made a few encouraging or deprecatory remarks, as seemed to be called for. She even found herself dancing, creditably enough, with him, then Charles again, then with her neighbor from across the table. No one seemed to think there was anything amiss about her. Indeed, one of her partners, gazing up at her slightly, asked her if she did any modeling and seemed incredulous at her hasty disclaimer. Everyone seemed to accept her at face value, as Tina Mallard, a rather tall, attractive girl. Even the stares of Sally Goddard and Suki McCormick as she passed them on the dance floor had no power to discomfit Tina that evening, but she was grateful to be spared another confrontation with Lilly.

By the time coffee and liqueurs had been served, Tina saw that it was past midnight. The car, she knew, had been ordered for twelve, and Fentiman would be waiting for them. Regretfully, Tina began to excuse herself to Charles, and to hasten to round up the girls for the return to Mallard Cottage.

"Don't leave yet, Tina," Charles requested. "Put the kids in the car and come back. I'll take you home."

But Tina had been put in mind of her own delinquency. She had been bidden to the dance to supervise the girls, and had been derelict in her duty, paying them only the most cursory attention as she whirled about the dance floor. Moreover, she was overcome with shyness at the thought of Charles taking her home. It was one thing to join him and his friends for dinner and dancing, but it seemed quite another to have him drive her home. Hurriedly she took leave of the others whom she had just met, and then, as Charles saw her to the car, shepherding the three girls before her, she said to him shyly, "Thank you so much, Charles. I never thought I'd have such a wonderful evening." Quickly, he seized her hand, and as she paused, he kissed her lightly on the cheek, and closed the car door behind them.

As soon as the car door was shut, the girls turned to Tina as one. "Well," drawled Leigh appreciatively. "You *have* been making the big time. We grossly underrated you, dear cousin."

Mimsi looked at her, a little worriedly. "I wonder if Mummy will be cross?"

Tina shared her apprehension. But Brooke bubbled, "Oh, but the entire evening with Charles Corbin! Tina's made! A success. Better late than never. Why this was practically your debut, Tina."

And, silently, Tina acquiesced. It had been exactly like a coming-out party for her. Her brief, disturbing encounter with Tony Corbin, whom she had failed to observe on the dance floor during the rest of the evening, was all but forgotten in the golden glow of pleasure she had felt in Charles's solicitous company.

Having seen the girls into their rooms and checked on the sleeping boys, Tina was preparing for bed. There was a knock on her door and Lilly entered the yellow room and sat down on the end of Tina's bed. "You seemed to have had a good time this evening," she remarked evenly.

Tina glanced at her shyly. "Yes, I've never had a more wonderful evening, Lilly. Thank you so much for the dress, and for insisting that I go," she said gratefully.

"Oh, don't mention it," Lilly replied dryly. "It's a change to see you looking so attractive. But I stopped in on my way to my room for a purpose, Tina. I must insist that you erase from your mind any idea of continuing your friendship with Charles Corbin."

"You don't want me to be friendly with Charles? Why not?"

Lilly seemed to hesitate. "For one thing, he's much too old for you."

And too young for you—Tina barely suppressed the retort which rose to her lips, and replied, instead, with what she thought was the undoubted truth. "Oh, he was terribly nice to me tonight, but I daresay he'll never even think of me again. He was just being kind, seeing that I was so out-of-things," Tina ventured.

"Yes, he can be very kind, when it occurs to him. Just see that you don't encourage him in future. It would be most unsuitable, believe me."

Tina couldn't help recalling Tony's warning that Charles was only dancing with her to spite Lilly. Tina responded wearily, "I'm sure it won't even arise, Lilly. But still, it's been a wonderful evening for me." And she sank down onto her bed next to Lilly and hesitatingly ventured a small kiss of gratitude on Lilly's cheek. Lilly stared at her for a moment, then rose and silently left the room, closing the door softly behind her. Tina sank back into her bed and, before she had finished recounting to herself the events of the evening, fell asleep.

Chapter 12

A brisk knock on her door awakened her far too early the next morning. It was Sunday, and one of the house rules was that on Sundays everyone breakfasted early together so as to ensure a full family turnout at chapel. Tina wondered to herself as she struggled awake to what extent the family maintained Sunday worship during the rest of the year but she knew she had no choice but to rise. The interdenominational chapel service was a regular feature of life on the island and Lilly's insistence on its observance was to be complied with.

Actually the weekly sermon by visiting ministers served more to entertain than to provoke spiritual qualms among the island's population, and the socializing that followed the brief service was at least as significant a part of it as the ritual. She duly presented herself for a perfunctory and drowsy family breakfast and drove off to chapel. There she was a little startled to note both Tony and Charles Corbin, with their parents, on an adjacent bench. But their presence was not really surprising, since the chapel was full and most of last night's other revelers were present, as well. She saw Sally Mallard with her five children, Suki McCormick seated with the Wigmore's, and some of her table companions of the night before. It was quite a turnout for a Sunday of the golf tournament weekend.

The sermon was mercifully brief, but the proceedings were prolonged pleasantly by several christenings which were to take place that morning. Cup Weekend had indeed brought the scattered multitude back to the island, and it had become a tradition among the old families to present the annual crop of offspring for this joyful ceremony in the chapel on the island. Tina watched, with some amusement, as the minister managed to formally bestow their future titles on three struggling infants of varying ages. Wardlow Williston, Kimberly Mildred Prosser, and Herrington James Harper had joined the ranks of island society.

They rose to leave and encountered the Corbin family in the aisle. Tina stole a glance at Lilly, but the latter, with her usual poise, was engaging the elder Corbins in cheerful conversation. Tina could not avoid greeting Charles, as well as Tony, but while their remarks were perfunctory, the Mallard and Hemmingway young had no similar inhibitions. Tony was a particular target for Goddard's attention, as they dove into conversation about the imminent Blackstone Cup regatta. That left Charles to Tina, the girls, and Finny. Tina was absurdly relieved when, after greeting each of them, Charles addressed himself to the youngest member of their party, asking Finny what he had been up to, and how his riding was coming. Finny visibly puffed with pride, proceeded to give Charles rather a full account of his equestrian prowess.

Progress up the aisle was halting, as similar groups blocked their egress. Tina, following directly behind Lilly, was forced to overhear her conversation with the Corbins. Mrs. Corbin was an elderly white-haired lady, whose slim figure was held erect almost to Tina's own height. She was enquiring graciously after the absent Findlay Hemmingway when her husband interjected with gallantry, "Lilly, you must be bored to tears being left alone all summer with a houseful on your hands. I don't know what that husband of yours can be thinking of. Bring them all over to our place this afternoon and I'll give you a good drink—one of my special daiquiris— and a stiff game of croquet."

Helen Corbin corrected her husband with amusement. "A beautiful girl like Lilly's never bored, dear— you're still a girl to us Lilly. What Kermit means is that *he's* bored and he wants someone new to take on and thrash at croquet. Do come, and bring the children. Sometimes Kermit and I feel rather isolated up on the Hill, with no grandchildren of our own to liven things up." She looked with mocking reproach toward Charles, who was about to step forth into the sunlight with Finny.

Little as this kindly offered invitation could have been agreeable to Lilly, Tina had to admire her poise. "Helen, you know I'd love to visit you, even though Kermit's croquet game is way beyond me. But I'm afraid I've already made plans for this afternoon."

"What a shame," Helen Corbin murmured. "But do send the children anyway. It will do Kermit a world of good and they'll enjoy it, too. And we must, of course, have Tina."

Lilly paused, but even her rapid wits were unequal to the invention of a previous engagement for all of them which her children would not hotly dispute. She gave way with good grace. "You're really too kind, Helen. I'm sure they'll make perfect nuisances of themselves."

"Nonsense," Helen Corbin answered easily, "it's just what they'll like. And they can use the pool, too, if it gets too hot on the croquet lawn. They won't be a bit of bother; Kermit will enjoy instructing them. We're just sorry that you can't come, but, of course, Tina will be there to keep them in order."

This second mention of her name seemed rather pointed to Tina. She began to wonder if this invitation was as spontaneous as it had seemed. Lilly, too, seemed to have noticed it, for she looked back at Tina over her shoulder hurriedly, but seemed to find no way out. "Then I'm sure they'd love it. I'll send them up around three, shall I?"

"If you're using the car, one of my boys can pick them up," Helen answered.

"No, no," Lilly demurred. "It will be perfectly convenient. Fentiman can bring them back around five thirty. So kind of you and Kermit. Thank you." And they parted.

The girls were half-hearted in their reception of the treat which lay ahead of them, although somewhat reconciled by the prospect of seeing the Corbin's Hill House which stood up on a cliff overlooking the ocean, far out on the road running from the village to the more outlying portions of the island. They could not recall having visited it before, as no contemporaries of theirs had ever been in residence. But Goddard and Finny were both visibly delighted. As for Lilly, she said little except to admonish them as to their behavior, but Tina could see that she was more than somewhat annoyed. Someone had prompted the Corbins' to extend this invitation and Tina couldn't help speculating as to whether it had been Tony or Charles.

The Corbin house, standing by itself on the dunes, far from the main road, was less imposing than the general run of island cottages, which tended toward a pre-World War I vastness of scale, but Tina's slight disappointment was soon overcome when she entered it and found that the interior, and then the grounds, demonstrated jewel-box perfection. Unlike the sprawling, dim interiors of Mallard Cottage, everything here shone in the sparkling light reflected from the ocean below. The furniture mingled the rich veneers of French antiquity with occasional pieces lacquered in white, and all was upholstered in a cheerful print of pink and white, the floors deeply carpeted in a grass-green. The house was obviously Helen Corbin's domain, while the velvety croquet lawn, of smoothly rolled perfection such as Tina had never dreamed could arise from the raw earth, was Kermit Corbin's precinct. The girls were rapidly engaged as novices by Kermit Corbin who proceeded to instruct his three prospects in the etiquette and technique of lawn croquet as it should be played. Finny and Goddard soon induced Charles and Tony—*both* of whom had been present to greet them—to show them the bath house and pool, located out of sight of the main house, partway down to the ocean. Tina found herself left to engage her hostess in conversation over a glass of lemonade on the deck overlooking the croquet lawn.

Helen Corbin seemed to resemble her son, Tony, while Charles was more like his huge, hearty father. She appeared elderly to Tina, but she was slim and attired in the delicate pastels of a Liberty frock which were becoming to her white hair. As she inspected Tina with a pair of vibrant blue eyes, Tina reached the conclusion that Mrs. Corbin was the dominating partner in this marriage. She certainly had orchestrated the visit so as to achieve her aim—an interlude with Tina.

Helen Corbin began in a gracious voice: "Well, my dear, at last we meet. Oh, don't look startled. I knew your grandparents, and your father, too, when he was the age of my Tony, and I've often wondered about you." Tina stiffened, poised to take offense, but Helen Corbin shrewdly observing her reaction said, "Now don't raise your hackles at me, my dear. I mean that most kindly. We've seen you about from time to time, you know, and you remind me more and more in appearance not only of your father, but of your grandmother who was the terror of island society when I was a young matron. You seem to have grown up quite nicely. But I've often felt things worked out unfairly, for you." Tina flushed. But Mrs. Corbin continued smoothly, leading the conversation down the path she had mentally marked out for it. "And we mustn't blame Lilly. She's had a difficult time of it. Nothing ever seems to quite work out for that girl, and yet, I can remember her as the lovely Lilly Goddard, setting every bachelor's head in a whirl, with the promise of everything life can give in store for her."

"Oh, no one would dream of blaming Lilly," Tina answered. "Lilly's always been kind to me. I know that she doesn't have to have me here at all. I used to think, when I was younger and romantic, that she invited me because, after all, I was her husband's child, and she'd loved him. But somehow, I don't think that any more," Tina confessed. She had the feeling that, under the older woman's shrewd but sympathetic gaze, she was blurting out thoughts and speculations which she had never meant to put into words. But her outspokenness did not seem to take Helen Corbin aback.

"Lilly never loved Skippy Mallard, my dear—nor he her," Mrs. Corbin answered her unarticulated question. "They married because both sets of their parents instructed them that it was the best thing for them to do. Lilly obeyed because she's never doubted the importance of the family, and your father, why, by that time I don't think he much cared."

Abandoning her usual caution, Tina asked, "Please, if you would, tell me about him. Nobody ever wants to talk about my father, except to tell me that I look like him."

"Well, you see, there isn't so very much to tell. He died so young you know." Helen Corbin reflected for a moment before saying, "The most exceptional thing about him was that, while he was very sweet, he was so absolutely ordinary. We were raised, my generation and his too, with the idea that family background, wealth, and the leisure that wealth brings, required us to achieve something. We thought that we were superior and that it was requisite that we demonstrate it; a sort of noblesse oblige. I suppose we were very conceited, but that sort of upbringing did turn out some exceptional men. I imagine that Skippy's problem was that, as he grew up, he found that his perceptions exceeded his abilities. Not that he was dull, oh, no, he just couldn't find anything that mattered to him at which he could excel. He was a fair tennis player, not a bad rider, an average golfer, and then, when he went away to school, he discovered that he was just a run-of-the-mill student. I suppose that crushed him—he'd been expected to shine at Yale, but he didn't. Worse still, he must have noted that some of the scaff and raff with whom he came in contact had better minds than he did. I'm afraid, though this may hurt you, my dear, that he dropped out of school and married your mother on a sudden impulse. Perhaps he sought to sink into the ordinary throng, as if he thought he might have been happier if he'd been born at that social level. But it didn't work out. His parents, while disappointed, were shocked at his marrying so young and to so ordinary and unsuitable a girl. They urged him to end the marriage, assuring him that the family would make provision for you. I'm afraid by that time, he was quite willing.

"Then, Lilly, who was a year or two older and still hadn't contracted the spectacular alliance her mother had expected, was told that she ought to marry Skippy. And, while it wasn't a brilliant marriage, it was entirely suitable. They were second cousins, they'd grown up together and liked each other, and it was hoped it would be the making of Skippy. Well, they were married, it wasn't long before Lilly had a daughter and then a son, and it wasn't long either before Skippy had drunk himself to death, out of boredom I suppose.

"He was a nice boy, but he never found himself, or maybe he couldn't live with what he found."

Tina was appalled. "That's so terribly sad. My poor father. To die so young, and for no reason at all."

"Perhaps that was it. He couldn't find any reason for living, so he died. Lilly, at least, has always had a reason for going on. Although, I'll confess to you, I'm no longer as sure as I once was that it's such a good one. With Lilly it's not mere ancestor worship, you know, although like the rest of us she can track down her descent from distinguished colonial forebears, and tell you just where all the family trees connect. She's been well indoctrinated with faith in family and her duty to continue to maintain it. The Mallards, Goddards, Hemmingways, all of the old families must survive—and survive in the station which God has ordained for them. I'd like to be able to share in her unshakable conviction. After all, it's the way I was brought up, too." Helen Corbin shook her head, and sighed. "Our credos were fine, in their time, but carried to excess, they've ruined a lot of lives. Still, I've tried to teach my boys to be proud of who they are, and to strive to excel. It's sometimes best to stick to the old standards, even when you have doubts, than to abandon them and be left with nothing at all."

It struck Tina that Helen Corbin's confidence in her was disquieting, as well as gratifying. It was true that she had been the eager recipient of most of Mrs. Corbin's information, but such revelations implied intimacy and conferred responsibility. How had it happened that she, who had been so resolved to remain independent, had been swept into yet another relationship of trust? Since she had commenced this summer visit, she had had confidences thrust upon her. Lilly, she knew, evoked her sense of duty by the trust she had placed in her; could it be that Helen Corbin, too, expected some result from this meeting? But what could Mrs. Corbin possibly want from her? And despite these speculations as to her possible motives, Tina couldn't help but feel strong sympathy for this older woman who, in telling her so much, was surely trying to communicate to Tina even more than she could bring herself to say.

When she could speak, Tina said, "Mrs. Corbin, thank you for talking to me like this. I've often wondered, but no one else has ever spoken of the past to me."

"I don't suppose many people would want to take the chance of making fools of themselves. But you know, you must school yourself to expect people to pour out their thoughts to you. You have an irresistibly earnest way of looking out at the world, as if searching for answers. It makes one want to try and supply them. I was wondering what sort of a person you had turned out to be. I'm glad that I've had this opportunity to get acquainted. And it's good to see that you've turned out so well, despite everything. Children never grow up just the way one expects, you know. Now, I've been awfully worried about Charles."

Tina was puzzled. "About your son, Charles? But he's the nicest man I've ever met. Everyone likes him. He's a wonderful person."

Helen Corbin smiled, pleased at Tina's naïve enthusiasm. "I'm so glad you like him. Of course he's very handsome, though I probably shouldn't say it, he has charming manners, and he's popular. But he's thirty, and he hasn't yet begun to make his life."

Tina was still perplexed at the older woman's concern. "I can't imagine anyone worrying about Charles, Mrs. Corbin. He makes other people so happy that I'm sure he must be happy too."

Helen Corbin smiled again. "Then I must be grateful for your reassurance." She felt she had accomplished her purpose, and changed the subject once more. "Now you must tell me, are you happy here on the island?"

"Yes," Tina answered quickly. "Oh, yes, I've never been happier."

"Well, that's very good. That's surely very good."

Their colloquy was at an end, for the girls and Kermit Corbin insisted that Tina join them. She resisted, urging that, as a mere beginner, she would be no addition to their game, but Kermit Corbin took the position that that was all the more reason to start to learn at once. Helen Corbin, calling on her to accede, murmured, "You see, that's Kermit's remaining form of excellence, and he does so love winning. Go ahead, the worse you are, the happier he'll be to teach you."

The afternoon sun beating down on them finally brought their match to an end, and Mr. Corbin laughingly escorted his harem down to the bath house by the pool where, after changing into suits, they revived themselves with a swim in the limpid waters. Tina was relieved to find that she was not singled out for attention either by Charles, or by Tony, who on his home grounds and before his parents demonstrated that he had, after all, some mastery over the requisites of polite conduct. The balance of their visit passed innocuously and when Tina led the way to the car at five thirty, all agreed that they had spent a very pleasant day.

So it was all the more shocking for Tina to find, on their return home, that Lilly was sitting in the living room, looking drawn and haggard, her shining hair in disarray, a half-empty drink and an ashtray full of cigarette ends showing that she had been under tension for some time. Lilly called out to her in a hoarse whisper, "Send the children upstairs to change for dinner Tina and come in here, please."

Tina sat beside her with some trepidation, wondering at Lilly's overwrought reaction to a casual and unavoidable social visit. She began to explain that, while Charles had been there, they hadn't even spoken alone, when Lilly interrupted her.

"Yes, never mind that now, Tina. I've had a cable, from my husband, from Findlay."

"Not bad news I hope, Lilly?"

Lilly laughed without humor. "Oh, no, there's nothing wrong with him. He's cabled from somewhere in the depths of Africa. Ougadougou, wherever that is. He's flying home. He expects to be here on Tuesday. That's the day after tomorrow."

Tina's face brightened. "But surely that's good news?"

Lilly looked at her, without seeming to see her. At last she replied, with a sigh, "Let's hope you're right. I'm going out. Make the arrangements please, Tina. Call the airport and find out when his flight is due, and see that Fentiman knows that he's to go to the airport. And tell Mrs. Chambers that Mr. Hemmingway will be here some time Tuesday. She'll know what to get in and how to arrange the menus. Tell her that I don't know how long he'll be staying."

Tina couldn't help feeling surprise at the tenor of these requests but she restrained herself from expressing it.

"Of course, Lilly. Why don't you take a rest, now? You're looking a little tired."

Lilly responded sharply, "I told you, I'm going out. Don't expect me for dinner, I may be back late. Oh, yes, there's one more thing. Have Hodges prepare the green room for Mr. Hemmingway." And Lilly abruptly tore out of the house.

Chapter 13

Tina saw little of Lilly the following day. Strangely enough she seemed to be keeping to her room, and even had her meals sent up on a tray.

The Tuesday of Findlay Hemmingway's expected arrival coincided with a break in what had been a spell of flawless summer weather. The skies dripped water, the interior of Mallard Cottage changed its aspect from one of welcoming dimness in contrast to the glaring sunlight outside, to a uniformly somber grayness deepening into shadows in the corners of the spacious rooms where no ray of artificial light reached. The air itself felt chill and dank as they huddled indoors. Finny was sulky because he was missing his riding; Goddard was downcast because a challenge race which he'd expected to win had to be canceled. The girls were merely bored and dejected at their unaccustomed confinement to the house, as Fentiman had left before dawn to drive all the way to Kennedy Airport to meet the flight on which Findlay Hemmingway was expected to arrive. Lilly still kept to her room.

With time the general despondency only deepened. It

struck Tina that their ostensible reasons for discontent merely masked a more deep-seated tension in those around her. She could scarcely recall exchanging more than a few words with Findlay Hemmingway on the rare occasions on which her visits had coincided with his presence at Mallard Cottage. Her most vivid recollection of him was of the effect he had on the others of the household; when he was in residence his comfort and convenience unquestionably came first. Finny, as his son and the baby of the group, had been the only one of the children to engage his attention; otherwise all of his time was spent with Lilly. Now, in retrospect, she wondered what his presence in the house had meant to Mimsi and Goddard. Brooke and Leigh, as cousins, could be relatively indifferent to the arrival of a mere uncle, but how did Mimsi and Goddard feel at the prospect of the return of their stepfather? Tina regretted that her absorption in her own situation had blinded her until now to the fact that there were others who might have been growing up in less than enviable circumstances. She looked with new awareness at her half-sister and brother who were seated together in a moment of unusual amity gazing out of a window at the driving rain. The advent of Findlay Hemmingway seemed momentarily to have brought them together.

Tina finally engaged her young relatives in a game of Monopoly, all but Finny who, after fidgeting about the room, at last settled into the window seat with a book where he managed to remain oblivious of the ill-tempers surrounding him. Tina longed to follow his example, but had to referee the inevitable disputes which arose as to the rules to be followed and as to various combinations against individual players constituting "unfairness." Try as she did, it seemed impossible to still the constant bickering. She found herself longing for Findlay Hemmingway's arrival, for anything to break the monotony of this uncomfortable day with its depressing chill. But it wasn't until after luncheon that they heard over the steady patter of rain the sound of wheels on the graveled driveway. In a few minutes the door was flung open, and there was the vaguely remembered figure of Findlay Hemmingway.

Tina saw before her in the entry a strongly made man, in his late fifties she conjectured, his gray hair thinned on top to expose a heavily freckled scalp. His naturally ruddy complexion was deeply tanned, and his movements vigorous as he jerked off his Burberry and thrust it at Fentiman, who followed closely behind him bearing two pigskin suitcases. With a cursory glance he took in the troop of young people who had filed dutifully out of the library to greet him and he shook hands briefly with each. Only Finny displayed genuine pleasure at his arrival. He had flung down his book and raced toward his father with a smile of greeting on his face, only to appear abashed as Findlay Hemmingway held him off for an instant of scrutiny and then, although with a smile, shook hands with him too. "You're growing up, young man," was his father's greeting to him, and Tina saw that it was accompanied by a brief pat on the head. She wondered at the lack of effusiveness of this meeting, after so long a separation, but remembered Lilly's remark that her husband had never really assumed the paternal role toward her own children. Naturally enough, Tina had thought. But even toward Finny his manner was unusually reserved and Finny appeared chagrined at what was almost a rebuff. The girls certainly were unwontedly subdued and Goddard had assumed his normal air of indifference.

Tina felt it incumbent on her to step forward to join the others. "I'm Tina Mallard, Mr. Hemmingway," she said shyly, offering her hand. "I've been staying here for the summer."

Cool gray eyes met hers appraisingly and, although he seemed a little unsure of exactly who she might be, he shook her proffered hand too. Then he enquired briskly, "Where's my wife? Where's Lilly?"

There was an instant of silence, so that Tina felt compelled to reply as none of the others volunteered. "She's upstairs in her room, Mr. Hemmingway. Perhaps she hasn't heard you arrive, what with the noise of the rain and wind."

Findlay Hemmingway did not comment but started to ascend, calling back as he did so, "Bring those bags up, Fentiman."

As he passed her, Tina spoke quietly to the chauffeur. "The green room, I believe."

The two men climbed the stairs as the group below looked up at their receding backs.

Now that the car was again available, Tina had the inspiration of driving into town for an ice cream at the coffee shop where the girls might possibly meet some friends. At least it would break up the dismals from which they had been suffering all day. Her suggestion was greeted with enthusiasm by Mimsi and the twins, and even the two boys seemed anxious to get out of the house, no matter what their destination. So when Fentiman descended they grabbed their slickers and, flinging them over their heads, ran through the pelting rain for the car.

Enough of the other summer colonists had felt impelled to escape their enforced solitude to make the Kraut's positively crowded at midafternoon. The juke box was playing and the smoky atmosphere inside the shop provided a sharp contrast to the gray sheen of empty sidewalks, and the choppy, wine-dark waves of the waters beyond. A sundae apiece soon brought each of them into a more cheerful frame of mind. The girls found friends already seated at tables and joined them. Tina frowned. Had she been wise to bring Goddard here? But the two half-brothers, Goddard and Finny, had found common ground in a discussion of whether or not the Labor Day weekend sailing races would have to be postponed and Tina was gratified to see Finny flush with pleasure as Goddard offered to let him crew for him a couple of days that week and see if he could make a sailor of him. Tina was touched by this rare fraternal contact between the two boys, and amused by the fact that Goddard's method of approach reminded her forcefully of how his idol, Tony Corbin, treated Goddard. Maria, her natural charms as much as ever in evidence, was being rushed off her feet, too busy with her duties for any prolonged conversation with anyone. What truth was there in Tony Corbin's tale, or had he merely been leading her on? While Maria's remarks had shown her to be simmering with ambition for "success," they were a far cry from the half-veiled innuendo, the cheap accusations Tony had made. Thinking of him, she was startled to find him standing behind her at the counter, bending down to get her attention.

"I saw your car pull up," he explained, using the back of his hand to wipe away the drops of moisture which clung to his sun-streaked hair and threatened to fall into Tina's face. She lifted her napkin to offer to him and he leaned lower. "You do it," he said, so she mopped at his long locks while he smiled at her.

"Okay, you're decently dry."

Tony stood up and took a brief look around the crowded room. "Phew, it's smoky in here. Finish up, and come over to the Yacht Club. At least the air is clean over there. I've been going through some tackle. Come and keep me company." Goddard looked up hopefully at Tony, but the latter frowned at him good-humoredly. "Not you, my boy—there's nothing more I can teach you in that line. You stay here and babysit Finny and I'll give you a dollar."

Finny protested, "I don't need a babysitter," but subsided as Goddard punched him lightly on the shoulder.

"Eat your ice cream," his brother told him.

Tina looked up at Tony. "I don't know if I can. Fentiman will be calling for us here in a little while."

"I'll drive you back later, if you miss him. Come on, Tina, don't you want to get out of all this noise and frowst?"

Tina left her money on the counter, and, pulling on her slicker, meekly followed Tony out the door. He held her arm as the force of the wind-driven rain struck them when they emerged onto the vacant sidewalk.

"Run," Tony shouted in her ear, and together they crossed the road, raced past the intervening automobiles parked in the Yacht Club lot, and pelted up the gangplank which led to the dry haven of the club itself.

"Here," Tony said, thrusting a large club towel at her. "Better mop up. You know, Tina, I was surprised you came. You always seem to be making excuses and running away from me."

"You know, Tony," she replied, rubbing her short curls briskly, "I was surprised you walked across the street to ask me. But I came because I've finally decided that your bark is much worse than your bite."

"But you aren't quite sure yet, are you?"

"Then I've decided to gamble for once. I was really glad to get away from my 'family,' this afternoon. We've had quite a day."

"Kiddies giving nursey a hard time?" Tony teased.

"Well, they have been getting under my skin," Tina replied. "They've been snapping at each other all day, being barred from their natural pursuits by this dismal weather. It's the kids and the whole atmosphere in the house ever since we came home for dinner Sunday and found out that Findlay Hemmingway was due back. Lilly's been practically invisible, and the air seems to seethe with tension. You'd think she'd be delighted to see her husband for a change. I really don't understand it."

"I didn't know Hemmingway was coming to the island this summer. When is he expected?"

"He's not expected, he's here. He went upstairs to greet Lilly, and we cleared out. Suddenly, I just wanted to get away."

"Whenever you feel that urge, come see me," Tony proposed.

Tina looked at him suspiciously. "You're being awfully nice to me, all of a sudden. Why the abrupt change?"

Tony laughed. "My technique didn't seem to be getting me anywhere. So I decided to take a leaf out of a master's book and try to win you with a more gentlemanly approach. And see, it worked. I called and you came."

"That sounds more like the old Tony to me," Tina snorted. "But if you mean do I prefer kindness to insults, yes I do."

"Then that shall be my policy," Tony assured her. "The leopard has changed his spots, the Ethiopian's skin is turning white right before your very eyes." He dangled a sunburned arm before her, inviting inspection, but she thrust it away.

Tina leaned back against the canvas cushions piled on the floor on which they'd been sitting. "You know it is nice and quiet and peaceful here. I'm glad you asked me to come over. Are you very busy?"

"On the contrary. With the race canceled, I've nothing to do all afternoon. I just came down here to get out of my house. Being shut up with Charles today was like being shut up with a squirrel on a treadmill. I've never seen him so edgy. He's driving us all out of our skulls."

Abruptly Tina asked, "Was it your idea to have your parents invite us out to the house last Sunday?"

"Nope. Not I," Tony said. "For some reason of her own my mother wanted to get to meet you. But it was Charles who suggested having all the kids up for the day. Odd, wasn't it?"

"But that was so like him. He's truly considerate. And

we liked it. Everyone had a good time, and I really enjoyed talking to your mother."

"She's a nice old thing, isn't she?" Tony agreed. "She's the one who approves of my going to medical school. My dad can't understand why I want to knock myself out in school training to spend my life with a lot of miserably sick people instead of going into the bank, like Charles."

"Oh, is that what he does?" Tina asked, curiously.

"Sure. It's traditional. He plays with trusts and administers estates, including ours as well as lots of our friends'. That's what Dad did too, before he retired. It's a good life, surrounded by the right kind of people, plenty of leisure, good vacations. A perfect job, if you have to fill up the time between holidays with something."

"But it didn't appeal to you?"

"No. Not that my father doesn't have me all wrong, too. I don't see myself as a medical missionary. But I do think that I'll find a challenge in medicine, and something I can be interested in learning and doing for the rest of my life."

"I know exactly," Tina agreed. "My mother can't see why I don't concentrate on finding someone who'll support me in the style to which she'd like me to become accustomed. But calculating parasitism somehow fails to appeal as a way of life. Take the women on the island; even the complainers like Suki McCormick are really satisfied that they've got it made, but it wouldn't satisfy me. They all seem the same, with nothing to talk about but each other. I'd have to have more than that on my mind, and for some reason unraveling the long buried past seems to call to me. But studying Mexican archaeology seems obstinately perverse to my mother—'You don't even meet any decent men in the field,' she keeps saying."

Tony kidded, "But I thought that was what was meant by the romance of archaeology. Aren't you giddily looking forward to the time when you can whisper, 'I'll meet you in the moonlight by the tomb, Cecil?' "

Tina giggled. "Well, hardly. You know better than that. Mostly it's poring over inscriptions, and there are literally millions of them which have yet to be deciphered. There's so much to be done, so much material already available and so little of it analyzed. And more sites are always being discovered. Remember, we're dealing with the remaining records of literate civilizations. Some of their predecessors may have far surpassed the Aztecs who borrowed from them. The Aztec civilization found by the conquistadores was already in a decline. And even what still exists of their relatively contemporaneous data isn't yet understood. Did you know that the Spanish at first deliberately destroyed all the written records of the Aztecs they could lay their hands on? Except for the work of one missionary, de Sahagún, nothing written would have survived the first impact of the conquerors. He died in 1590, but even today not all of his manuscripts, setting down what existed in Mexico at the time, have been translated from the Aztec language in which he wrote."

"And you really want to devote your life to puzzling out the meanings of records in a dead language about a vanished people?" Tony asked seriously. "Why?"

Tina eyed him doubtfully. "I don't know whether I can make you understand. It's a challenge, like a crossword puzzle perhaps, when you know that someone terribly clever has set up the clues. They're all there; if only you have enough time and enough intelligence and, more important, sympathy with the mind of the person who constructed the puzzle, you can solve it."

"But suppose you ponder over some long screed and then discover it's only the equivalent of an ancient laundry list? I can't see much gratification in that."

"Well, at the least it would show that they sent out their laundry and what kind of clothes they wore. But I don't believe that any people would take the trouble to elaborately incise trivia in stone. And, of course, I've got a hypothesis; it wouldn't be as interesting without a hypothesis, I grant you. I think that careful study of everything we can find that has been left by the ancient Mexicans will demonstrate that their civilizations did not develop in complete isolation from the rest of the world. For years the chief credo of archaeological investigators was that these states developed their amazing religion and technology without any contact with Europe, Asia, or Africa. But now it's beginning to be shown that the Middle-American cultures were influenced by diffusion—from Indonesia and Japan, by way of South America, and perhaps even from Europe and Africa. There's always been speculation by amateurs that the huge pyramids of the Toltecs at Chichén Itzá and of the Mayas at Uxmal and Palenque might have some relationship with Egypt. Archaeologists used to scoff at such theories because the Middle-American pyramids didn't have the same function as the Egyptians'. But then a pyramid-tomb was found at Palenque. It's more reasonable now to investigate whether there might have been a central source influencing both cultures, or at least whether there could have been diffusion from the Old World to the New. I would opt for the Phoenicians. They were great sailors. It also seems plausible the same harsh world-view would have inspired the religions of human sacrifice we know were practiced both at Carthage and by the Aztecs and their predecessors.

"It's so fascinating to me that I don't see how anyone could dismiss archaeology as the study of dusty old pots. I've got to manage to finish college and find work in the field. I don't know how I'll do it, but I must."

Appalled by the length and intensity with which she had held forth, Tina looked at Tony in sudden embarrassment and began to apologize. "I'm sorry, Tony. I didn't mean to gush over like that. I don't expect you to be interested in my stupid problems."

"Why not? If we're going to be friends, then we don't always have to keep it light, do we?"

Tina gazed at him. "Are we going to be friends, Tony?"

Without answering, he put his arm around her and drew her head onto his shoulder. Her still damp hair tickled his ear.

"Will you kiss me, Tina?" he whispered.

Shyly, she turned her face and placed her lips gently against his. He made no move toward her for a moment but accepted what she had given and then took her into the circle of his arms. They sat still, together, without speech, while the rain pounded on the roof and beat at the plate-glass windows.

Tina finally drew herself away from his embrace with a little sigh. "You're very surprising to me, Tony. You're not at all like what I thought you were." She rose to her feet and reaching her hand down to him pulled him up.

Tony stood beside her, then drawing her attention to the darkened sheet of glass before which they stood, said, "Look at the window. What do you see?"

Their blurred reflections met her curious gaze, two figures alike in size and shape, appeared almost like twins to her startled eyes. "Is that really us?"

"Tina and Tony."

She stared, transfixed at their nearly identical images. Suddenly she blurted out, "Oh, Tony, I've got to go. I really must get back to the cottage and see what's happened."

"Don't go," Tony urged. "Stay here with me. You don't really have to leave, Tina. You're running away from me again."

"But I must get back," Tina argued. "The children, Lilly, they may need me. I don't understand what's happening but it was easy to see that everyone has been put in a state by Mr. Hemmingway's arrival. And he seemed so withdrawn and strange, too. Oh, I don't know what I was thinking of, I shouldn't have stayed away all this time. I must get back."

Tony answered reluctantly. "I did promise to drive you home, didn't I? But I didn't say when."

"Oh, Tony, don't tease me now. I can't stay, I can't."

"Can't, or don't want to? It doesn't really matter, does it?" He was very angry.

"Tony, really, I must go back," she pleaded.

"All right," he rejoined, with a return of his usual flippancy, "if all you need is a chauffeur, I'm your man. This way, my lady."

Tina was miserable. He couldn't or wouldn't understand the sudden feeling of apprehension, arising only in part from guilt at responsibility evaded, that directed her back to the cottage. But mixed with her misery was a tiny feeling that her impulse would not have been quite so urgent if she hadn't been afraid to stay here with Tony, afraid to remain in the quiet and warmth of this refuge from the elements any longer. And her fear was no longer of Tony Corbin, but of herself.

The short trip was made in silence until Tony stopped the car in front of the entrance to the cottage. Tina said softly to his profile, "I'm sorry you're angry with me, Tony. Truly, I am." Then she raced through the rain for the front door.

The house was still, the entrance hall deserted. But, as she took note of the time on the grandfather clock which faced her, Tina started for the stairs. She'd have to hurry to change, if she wasn't going to be late for dinner.

Chapter 14

Lilly made a resplendent appearance at the dinner table that evening. Her hair was drawn back again in gleaming yellow coils, pearl and jade circlets in her ears emphasizing her deep tan, and she appeared cool and poised in her crisp green-and-white silk dress. Tina found herself seated on the right of Findlay Hemmingway, at the other end of the table. Goddard sat opposite her. Glancing around the dining room, Tina was again struck by the sheer physical good looks which were represented. Findlay Hemmingway, though well into middle age, epitomized the word "fit"; Goddard, opposite her, was growing tall and, taking after his mother in features, gave promise of an almost classic handsomeness as soon as the softened curves of adolescence give way to more masculine firmness. Mimsi and the twins looked like a page out of *Town and Country*, each pair of blue eyes set in a deeply tanned oval and framed by long silky hair differing only to a degree in shade of fairness. Even Finny, though gangly in the in-between stage between boy and youth, appeared remarkably attractive to her; his dampened hair brushed back into neatness appeared like streaked honey over his bright eyes, as his long lean face constantly turned toward their end of the table on the alert to catch the least word let fall by his father. Findlay Hemmingway was holding forth in a way which had commanded their attention, describing his trip through Africa. Landing in Morocco, he had worked his way—mostly by Land Rover, interspersed with short hops by airplane, and occasional trips on foot—through Algeria, Libya, Chad, the Sudan, Uganda, Kenya, and Tanzania and then flown to the West Coast to begin a survey of the former French West African states. He had crossed the Serengeti-Mara plains, and inspected Kenya's Tsavo Park, where the concentration of elephants in the protected area had resulted in the almost complete destruction of the range all along the rivers. His conclusions were not sanguine.

"We have to keep a close eye on those fellows," he opined. "Of course, they're dealing with population pressure, but they're just local politicians; they give way to the short-run solution, and they let their people overgraze the savanna and clear the land for farming. The country won't support more people living that sort of life. After a few years—at most, decades—the moisture is gone, the plant life weakened or depleted, and it turns to desert. The destruction caused a century ago by the Boers in the South African veldt is being repeated now throughout Africa. Of course, since the General Assembly in Nairobi in '63, there has at least been organized concern. But not much progress. In the meantime, the first sufferers are the animals. The wildlife disappears and it can't be replaced. They've got to be reminded that some of these specimens are unique to Africa; if they're wiped out, they're lost to the world. Why, at Aberdare in Kenya they may let the Kikuyu cut the preserve into farms, and to hell with the elephants, rhino, and buffalo!"

Tina couldn't help but ask, "But what should they do

with the people, Mr. Hemmingway? Apparently they have to find some place to graze their herds or to farm." Findlay Hemmingway favored her with a hard look, then answered, "The trouble is, there are already too many of them. What these local chaps have got to keep in mind is that it's animals that are unique."

No one else at the table seemed disposed to query further, so Tina held herself in check. Lilly, however, appeared to have perceived the possibility of dissension at the other end of the table for she interjected, by way of explanation, "Tina, you see, has had three years of college." Continuing, Lilly said to Tina, "But I didn't know that Africa interested you. I thought that Mexico was your area." Hemmingway looked at her inquiringly.

"I'm not working with live things," Tina said. "I'm studying the relics of dead civilizations, the vanished Zapotecs, Toltecs, and Olmecs."

"Pots and figurines, that it?"

"Yes, and temple architecture and calendar stones."

"Is that so? Where are you studying?" he asked.

"I'm at Hunter College. I hope to be able to finish up, but of course I'll be twenty-one before the end of my senior year."

"So?" he enquired.

Tina was embarrassed. Hesitantly she brought out, "You see, the trust—the money I get—stops when I come of age."

Lilly looked at her, wonderingly. "But I hadn't realized, Tina. You mean that's all you have, isn't it? It never occurred to me before."

Tina nodded, uncomfortably. She certainly hadn't meant to display her relative poverty before them all at the dinner table. It looked as if she were asking for money.

Lilly spoke brightly, "I'll talk to the trustees. Surely we can work out something. It never occurred to me that anyone in the family could be concerned about money. That doesn't seem right."

Tina let this pass without comment. In the ensuing pause, Hemmingway's attention focused on Finny. "And what have you been busy with this summer, Finny?" he asked. "Your mother tells me you've been having tennis and swimming lessons, at day camp, as well as your riding. I'll have to come over and watch you at work one morning."

Finny gulped, visibly. "I really like the riding best, Dad. I'm not too keen on games."

"That's nonsense. This is the best time to get into the swing of it, Finny. You may feel awkward at first, but persevere. Play hard with these fellows and you get to know them; they'll be your friends for life. Competing against someone is the best way to cement the bonds of friendship." Finny looked dubious but didn't argue. Findlay Hemmingway continued. "No need to ask about the rest of you young people. Goddard, of course, sails, that and nothing else. The girls, well, it's obvious when I look at you. You're growing to be the image of Lilly." He gave them a look which contrasted strangely, Tina thought, with the benign meaning of his words. But the tone in which they had been uttered held scarcely veiled contempt. What in the world did Findlay Hemmingway have against his stepdaughter and nieces?

They glanced at Lilly, uncomfortably, who answered her husband coldly. "Yes, they've been very good girls, no trouble at all since Tina's been here."

"Oh," her husband picked her up. "Was there some trouble before that?"

Lilly hesitated. "We did have an au pair with us at the beginning of the season who seemed to do nothing but make difficulties. But since I dismissed her, all has been quite serene."

"Handled with your usual efficiency," Findlay Hemmingway commented dryly. Turning to Tina, he remarked, "Your presence seems to have been very salutary. I hadn't realized before how very fortunate we should count ourselves at having you available. Allow me to congratulate you on having made yourself indispensable to Lilly."

Tina writhed miserably as the thrust of his remark struck her. She was sure that, in the light of her earlier disclosure of her need for money, he had now classified her as a calculating schemer. She gave no answer but addressed herself to her plate. Really, now that she had had the benefit of his conversation at a meal, she didn't wonder that Lilly and the others had dreaded his arrival. With a few words, he had managed to make each person at the table thoroughly uncomfortable. She longed for dinner to end, and at long last, it did.

Lilly and Findlay Hemmingway left to commence an almost obligatory series of calls on their numerous relations who, it seemed, could hardly wait to congratulate Findlay on having managed to return to the island before the end of the season. When the telephone rang after nine that evening, Tina quite naturally took the call. At first when she heard a man's voice she thought it might be Tony, but on the instant her surmise was corrected.

"This is Charles Corbin. . . ."

"Charles, how nice!"

"Tina?"

"Yes."

There was a brief pause before Charles asked, "Are you all alone over there?"

She smiled to herself. "Not alone with three girls and two boys and a television set for company."

After a brief silence, he said, "Tina, how would you like to come out for a drive?"

"What, in this rain?" she asked, without letting her surprise and pleasure at his choice of her show.

"It's clearing, I promise you," he assured her. "We'll take a spin out to the cliffs. Have you seen the waves breaking on the cliffs after a storm? It's unforgettable. Do come."

Tina found the invitation irresistible. She raced upstairs to fix her face and hair and put on something casual but more attractive. She settled on a rose-colored turtleneck pullover, tucked into beige hip-huggers, applied her makeup carefully, as her cousins had so painfully instructed her, and, on an impulse, borrowed a pair of gold drops for her ears from Mimsi. Inspecting her reflection carefully in the brilliant light, she mentally compared it with the rain-bedraggled image of herself she had gazed at that afternoon at the Yacht Club with Tony. She shook the vision from her mind. Taking her raincoat to be safe, she was ready when Charles drove up in his Maserati, with the top fastened down for protection from the wind and the drizzle still falling.

Charles helped her into the car, then asked her, "How are things with you on this dreary day, little girl?"

Tina laughed. "You're the only one who can call me that!"

Charles laughed, too. "You're tiny Tina to me."

Tina thought to herself how nice it was to be given the feeling of being small and helpless by a man.

"Do you like to go fast?" Charles asked.

"I don't mind," Tina replied.

"It's the only way to drive. No one will be out on the island tonight. I can let go."

Charles spun the wheels as they left the graveled driveway and Tina felt their speed increase, the illusion of racing increased by the noise of the wind which buffeted them as the car took off down the narrow road toward the eastern shore of the island. Tina shrank down into the taupe suede bucket seat. Conversation was impossible against that background, even if Tina had dared to distract Charles's eyes from the road. A glance at the leather dashboard enclosing the speedometer showed that they were traveling at a mere ninety, and while Tina steeled herself to prevent any outcry from escaping her, she saw that Charles looked not only intent, but exhilarated. The end of the island was not far, at this speed, and she was thankful when Charles brought the car to a stop at the wooden barrier that prevented wheeled vehicles from attempting to descend the dirt track which knifed down the dunes to the beach below.

As Charles had foretold, the drizzle had lightened to a fine mist. They picked their way down the muddy path to the beach, and stood at the end of it. Tina saw that the fine sandy beach had been foreshortened by the monstrous rollers breaking far inshore from their normal cresting point. The spray from the ever-recurring surf mingled with the moisture-laden air and dampened her hair. She clutched Charles's arm. The fury of the ocean was indeed unforgettable. Its violence called forth a sympathetic reaction in both of them. Casting caution to the winds, Tina slipped out of her shoes and accompanied by Charles she darted forward to meet the foaming waters.

A dash of icy spray on their faces broke the wild mood of excitement and, still laughing in reaction to their impromptu dousing, they tore back to the shelter of the tiny car.

Charles's mood had lightened, as had her own. "Isn't this terrific!" Charles exclaimed. Tina agreed. The salt spray misted the windshield, even at that height, but they could still make out the white caps of the rollers crashing onto the shore beneath them. Charles turned to her. "That was what I needed. At least this day isn't a total loss." Tina nodded, and then Charles seized her and kissed her urgently; to her surprise Tina responded with urgency to match his own. The violent contrast between the abandon of the scene before them and the oppressive tension under which she had spent the day, and, even more oddly, the brief interlude with Tony that afternoon, seemed to combine to release all the inhibitions with which she had circumscribed her emotions.

The sudden intensity of their kiss shook both of them. Charles drew back from her, startled at himself. "You are such a dear little girl, Tina. I didn't mean that. Forget it."

Tina recoiled. "Do you mean I'm too young? I'm not really a 'little girl.' "

"No, not that. If anything, it's that I'm too old."

"I don't understand you," Tina murmured.

"I never meant to kiss you," Charles said. "Try to understand. You're very sweet; but I don't want to make love to you." Tina shrank into herself at these words. He continued, without pausing. "I asked you to come on impulse, but for quite another reason." Tina tried to make out his expression, but in the darkness of the car's interior, all she could see was his profile as he stared through the fogged glass in front of him. He continued. "I wanted to know, I had to know what's happening— between Hemmingway and Lilly?"

"Lilly? Lilly," Tina repeated in a strained voice. Her thoughts were in turmoil, yet her mind was working at high speed. With revulsion, she finally brought out, "You don't mean that you and Lilly . . . that you're having an affair?"

Charles laughed mirthlessly. "No, we're not having an affair, in that sense. We aren't sleeping together." He paused before continuing. "I was in love with Lilly once, but that was a long time ago. But I still care for her; I care very much about what's happening to her. She's confided in me; she doesn't know why her husband's returned so suddenly, and she's afraid."

"And that's why you asked me out here? To find out how Lilly is?"

"I'm sorry I've hurt you," Charles answered, shaking

his head. "It's been such a hell of a day. I didn't expect that you would pick up the telephone when I called. I didn't plan on anything, believe me, Tina."

Tears rose to her eyes, involuntarily. "I am a fool," she said softly.

"No," Charles replied, "you're a very sweet young girl. I'm the fool. I know that I'm at fault."

"Do you mean about Lilly?" Tina asked.

"Yes, Lilly, everything, the whole mess. I should never have listened to her, I should never have let time go by until it came to this."

Tina struggled unsuccessfully to keep her resentment out of her voice. "Well, as to Lilly, she's just fine. She's nobody's fool at all, unlike us. She's gone out quite happily to pay a round of visits. You know, have a drink with assorted Goddards, Hemmingways, Wigmores, the whole crowd. They're celebrating Findlay's return, after all. She didn't seem to me to be frightened of anyone."

Charles was visibly relieved, but then muttered half aloud, "I hope she knows what she's doing."

Tina's laugh was brittle. "I'm sure she knows; she always knows, haven't you noticed? Lilly's always in control, of all of us. I think you'd best take me home now, if you'll be so kind."

"Tina, it's you who've been kind, more than you want to believe. I'm truly sorry to have hurt you. I'll take you back now."

As silently as before, the Maserati raced through the night and Tina returned to the cottage, humiliated and resentful both, over Charles, although her anger was abated by his obvious unhappiness.

She crept quietly into the house and tried to make her way noiselessly up the steps to the safety of her room to nurse her misery in privacy. But before she could reach sanctuary, she was appalled to hear a muffled scream and the sound of a brutal slap. Lilly ran through the half-opened door of her room but stopped short on seeing

Tina. Seizing her by her sodden shirt, Lilly clutched Tina's arm. Tina looked at her in consternation; one side of her gleaming coiffure had fallen loose and dangled over a cheek which already showed the purpling imprint of the blow Tina had heard. As she struggled to take in this sudden apparition, Findlay Hemmingway loomed in the doorway, framed in the roseate glow of the organza hangings of Lilly's bedroom. He surveyed his cowering wife. He was unruffled, still clad in blue blazer and tie, his hands now thrust into his trouser pockets. The only sign he betrayed of what was obviously a violent scene was the heightening of the already ruddy color of his complexion. Without taking heed of Tina's presence, he spoke deliberately. "Come back here, Lilly. I won't hit you again. If only, for once in your life, you could bring yourself to be honest, my dear."

Tina felt a shudder pass through Lilly's delicate frame. Then, taking hold of herself, she faced her husband, still without relinquishing her grasp of the wet fabric of Tina's shirtsleeve. "I won't be alone with you again, Findlay."

"Oh, by all means, if you need moral support, and if you're sure that you won't later regret having a witness to our conversation, bring her in, too. As I said at dinner, she seems to have made herself quite indispensable."

Tina was bewildered. There was nothing she wanted less than to be present at a marital quarrel between Lilly and Findlay Hemmingway, but Lilly would not relinquish her hold, and Tina allowed herself to be drawn along into the rose room.

Findlay Hemmingway politely shut the door behind the two women. Addressing himself with ironic courtesy to Tina, he began to explain, as if for her benefit: "My wife, you see, has become so inured to hypocrisy, that she can't comprehend me when I tell her that she must and shall be honest with me this once, and she'll not regret it. Surely that's quite reasonable. But, I'm afraid I lost my temper at her inability to understand my simple request." Turning to Lilly, he asked, still in the most rational of tones, "Now, surely, you must see, I mean what I say. I haven't flown halfway around the world to be fobbed off with another of your evasions. I know the truth, but I expect to hear it from you. Is he, or is he not my son?"

Tina's gaze shifted rapidly from Hemmingway's face to Lilly's. Lilly remained silent. Then, tossing back her disarranged and dangling hair, she lifted her face to confront him.

"Well, what does it matter if, as you say, you know the truth?"

"Come, come, Lilly. I said no more evasions. Did you think I would spare you, because you dragged this girl in here with you? I want the truth from you, in your own words."

"Very well, then. Have it your way, as you obviously mean to. Is this what you're so anxious to hear? Finny's my son but not yours. As you've surmised, Charles Corbin is his father."

Tina uttered a low cry. Hemmingway's attention focused on her for a moment. "Let her go now, Lilly. There's no reason for her to remain. I promised you wouldn't regret it if you dealt with me honestly."

Tina felt Lilly's grip on her relax, and she fled from the room.

Stripping the clammy garments from her chilled body, Tina was overcome with a feeling of nausea. She sat on her bed and put her swimming head down on her knees. Finally, the violent shaking fit which had overtaken her stilled and she was able to draw her nightdress over her head and lie back on the pillow. But sleep was far away. Her thoughts were in a whirl, and hideous feelings of revulsion and shame, for herself, for having been a witness to this confrontation, and for Lilly, and for Charles, gave her no peace. Toward morning, as the light began filtering in through the drawn curtains, she finally fell into an uneasy slumber.

Chapter 15

Tina dragged herself from her bed late the next morning. She was unwilling to leave the sanctuary of her room. For an instant she clutched the hope that she had dreamed last night's encounter between Lilly and Findlay Hemmingway, but she knew it was untrue. She dared not speculate on what had transpired after she had left them together. She only knew that she could not bear to face either of them again. And Finny, she thought, what of poor Finny? What would happen to him now? Would he have to learn the truth? For it was the truth, Tina was convinced of it. Easy, in retrospect, to discover why Finny, who bore no particular resemblance to either of his nominal parents, had been called to her mind when she first met Tony Corbin. Simple, now, to understand why Charles had been overwrought. Lilly's dread of her husband's unexpected return from abroad was explained.

She had been totally deluded; that there might be elemental strains in the fabric of their life of gracious ease had never occurred to Tina. She had failed to decipher the meaning of obscure actions which she had observed but not appreciated. She had thought to be the independent but percipient viewer of the lives about her. Instead, she had become a participant in all too many relationships with little understanding of what was really transpiring. And worse. However little she now found that she had understood, the truth was that she had come to care. Perhaps she could physically withdraw from this ugliness and the distress which would surely ensue, but if she had this choice, she could not take it. Resolutely, Tina discarded the reflexive instinct to escape from entanglement. No matter how the others in the family might view her relationship to them—she acknowledged her ties, both of obligation and, in most cases, affection.

Tina hurriedly scrambled into her clothes and went downstairs, not knowing what she would find awaiting her.

To her dismay, the first person she encountered was Finny, seated on the bottom step of the stairs, patient but woebegone. Tina made an effort to appear cheerful. She asked if he had breakfasted and when he nodded enquired with assumed calm if everyone else had finished too. Finny's answer reassured her that he was as yet untouched, but gave warning that the storm still impended.

"Dad's still not down. I've been waiting and waiting. He promised to take me riding this morning, but it looks like mother and he are never going to get up." Tina toyed with the idea of trying to find Goddard and inducing him to take Finny out sailing instead. It might be best if the boys were out of the way, and yet she knew that she would have great difficulty in persuading Finny to abandon his vigil and was doubtful that Goddard would consent. Still, she asked Finny if he knew where his brother was. Finny's response raised still a new source of anxiety. "He cut out right after breakfast. Goddard never stays home when my Dad's here." A frown creased Finny's freckled forehead. "Tina, do you think he might be jealous? I mean, after all, he doesn't have any father, and I do, even if mine isn't around all that often." Seeing the expression on Tina's face, Finny apologized. "Oh, gee. I guess I shouldn't have said that to you. Mother's explained that he was your father too. I just forgot." Wordless, Tina rested her hand on his shoulder. At this reassuring gesture, Finny brightened. "But, if you want the girls, they're in the sun room. And guess who's come to call? Maria."

All thoughts of breakfast vanished from Tina's mind as she crossed the library into the sun room. Mimsi, Brooke, and Leigh sat, side by side, on a wicker sofa confronting Maria who occupied the matching arm-chair. The anxious look with which Mimsi greeted her entrance gave way to one of relief as she recognized Tina. Tina could tell that Mimsi was aware that something was amiss, and what one knew they all knew. In contrast, Maria reclined in the chair at her ease. No longer clad in the orange sateen uniform of duty, she had dressed herself for the morning call in a clinging jersey and pink stretch pants. Her manifest attractions no longer seemed to Tina to radiate wholesomeness and simplicity. Maria seemed to be extracting too much pleasure at the awkwardness of the situation and her appearance at the cottage this morning could not have been more ill-timed. Tina knew that she ought to make an attempt to dislodge her.

"This is a very early hour for a visit, Maria. Perhaps you might come back at another time?"

Maria was unfazed. "I have not been invited back for a little visit, so I had to choose my own time. Mr. Hemmingway has after all returned, has he not? Then I will wait to see him. Or Mrs. Hemmingway. Either one. It does not matter to me. Perhaps, after all, it would be better if she saw me."

Tina explained carefully: "Neither of them has break-fasted as yet, Maria. It would be best, I'm sure, if you made an appointment on another day, and perhaps you should telephone first. If there should be some particular subject you wish to discuss, some question about wages or a reference, you might tell me and I will take it up with Mrs. Hemmingway. But this is really not a convenient time for you to pay us a call."

"There is a particular subject, yes." Maria appeared amused but unmoving. "I will wait."

Tina shrugged and told the girls, "I think we must leave Maria to entertain herself."

They followed Tina to the breakfast room, passing Finny, who was still steadfastly lying in wait at the foot of the stairs.

"I have got to have a cup of coffee, after that," Tina admitted. "Really, Maria is the oddest girl. What could have possessed her to come back after all these weeks, on this of all mornings?"

Brooke unexpectedly replied to her rhetorical question. "Exactly. That's why we were sitting with her; we wanted to keep an eye on her. If she sees Uncle Findlay, she'll make trouble. Can't you get rid of her?"

Tina was exasperated. God knows, she agreed, there was already enough trouble in the house, but she had done her best. She was dismayed by Brooke's expressed forebodings and by her own inability to cope. She asked sharply, "Would you mind confiding in me as to what sort of trouble you anticipate Maria could make?"

Leigh asserted, "She's his spy, don't you see? He planted her here to get evidence for a divorce. That's why we were so glad when Lilly got up the courage to get rid of her." She sighed. "We were rather hoping that it would all blow over, but judging by the row last night, I suppose that's too much to hope for." She put her arm consolingly about her cousin Mimsi's shoulders.

Tina was appalled. "Do you mean you've known all this time, all summer? . . ." Her voice trailed off. She asked, "How much did you overhear last night?"

Mimsi had tears in her eyes. "It's not that we were eavesdropping. But of course we've been terribly concerned. Poor mother. It was just awful before he went away, and then, last night, we'd have had to be deaf not to know they were at it again."

"But you didn't hear any of the conversation?" Tina pursued.

Mimsi shrugged. "You don't have to hear the words to know when they're quarreling. It's so ghastly for Mummy. They used to be so happy. Then the arguments began. She's been absolutely unhinged all summer. We've been over it and over it, but none of us can imagine what went wrong, can we?" She looked at the twins for confirmation. "Maybe he's just going through that stage men go through. But it's simply terrible for mother. You know she absolutely adores him."

Tina could only stare at them openmouthed. Never in the weeks they had spent together had she seen the girls as other than gilded simpletons, too engrossed in their own youth and pleasure to spare a thought for anyone else's problems. She asked, "But Maria. You think she was planted here to spy on Lilly?"

Leigh answered, "But of course. Why else should she turn up now? And, if you had seen the way she went snooping about the house when she was here. And the things she used to ask us."

"What things?" Tina asked.

"All sorts of personal things," Brooke said. "About Lilly, ourselves, our guests. Everything was grist to her mill. I just wish we could get her out of here, now."

Tina thought for a moment, then said, "Since she doesn't seem inclined to take a hint, and I don't suppose we could ask Fentiman to carry her out, we may just as well let her sit there. She may get bored." In light of the revelation of the night before, Tina doubted that anything Maria could report to Findlay Hemmingway could make things worse.

Unable to face solid food, Tina was drinking her second cup of coffee when the four of them heard a heavy tread crossing the dining room.

Findlay Hemmingway pushed open the swinging door and entered with Finny at his heels. He looked at their faces, then at his wristwatch. "Late hours being kept around here, I see," was his greeting to them. The girls rose hastily as if to flee, but Hemmingway prevented them from leaving with a gesture. Tina had remained frozen over her coffee cup, unwilling to meet his eyes. Hemmingway appeared unperturbed by her obvious discomfiture.

"Just as well to catch you all together," he announced. He helped himself to juice from the pitcher on the sideboard, then searched about him in annoyance. "Where's my breakfast?" he demanded of the room at large. They stared back at him. He laughed mirthlessly to himself. "I did think that in my own home my days of roughing it would be over. But let Lilly take one late morning, and there's no one to trouble to make provisions for my needs." He turned to Finny. "Here, son, go find the cook and tell her I want my breakfast, at once. And while you're there, tell her to make up a tray for your mother."

As Finny hastened off to do his bidding, Hemmingway addressed the girls and Tina. He made an effort to infuse his voice with geniality as he said, "You're all big girls, and you have Tina to look after you. There'll be no problem if you have to manage on your own for a few days," he assured them. "Lilly seems to think she has to take care of everyone, but I told her that it's about time she let you do a little managing for yourselves. She has to put herself first, sometime. We'll be leaving for Africa this evening, Lilly, Finny, and I. We'll land at Accra and go on to finish the survey of West African conditions. A man's entitled to have his wife with him, after all. You'll all be fine here without her, won't you? It's just for a few days."

Tina hardly knew how to absorb this announcement. The girls were no less dumfounded, but Mimsi made the first recovery. "Why that's super! Just super! What fun for Mother and Finny. We'll manage perfectly well. Don't worry about us for a moment." Her cousins echoed her in confused enthusiasm which seemed to gratify Hemmingway. Only Tina remained silent.

The door to the kitchen opened and a flustered Mrs. Chambers appeared bearing a platter of scrambled eggs and sausages with hot toast. The sight of his approaching breakfast set the seal on Findlay Hemmingway's restoration to equanimity. Ruffling Finny's hair he said, "No time for riding today, I'm afraid. You've packing to do instead. But we'll make up for it once we're in Africa. Will that suit you?" Finny appeared enraptured at the prospect.

Mrs. Chambers asked timidly, "Hodges is out sir. Do you want me to take Mrs. Hemmingway's tray up to her?"

Findlay Hemmingway eyed Tina's downcast countenance appraisingly. "Would you mind taking the tray up, Tina? I think that Lilly would like to have a few words with you alone."

Automatically, Tina rose, took the tray from Mrs. Chambers, and began the ascent to Lilly's room. The bitter, impassioned Findlay Hemmingway of the previous night had been transmuted into the heavy-handed diplomatist. Would Lilly, too, have changed out of all recognition? Events had passed her ability to comprehend them.

She tapped lightly on the closed door to the pink room, and a cheerful voice bode her enter.

Lilly was partly dressed, standing near the bed, surrounded by clothes which had been pulled out of closet and wardrobe and cast down on bed and chairs. She smiled engagingly at Tina who stood fast in the doorway and took the breakfast tray, clearing a corner for it on her dressing table. Waving in the direction of the multiple garments swathing the furniture, Lilly announced, "I'm packing. I'm going back to Africa with Findlay, and he says he has to return at once."

"I've heard," Tina answered. "You and Finny." Her words seemed to reverberate between them.

Lilly sighed. "I won't ask you to forget what you heard last night, Tina. That wouldn't be possible would it?" Lilly said slowly as she pulled up a chair and sat down. "I'm sure I can rely on you and what you owe your family to let it go no further."

"Don't, Lilly," Tina mumbled. "You don't have to. Don't."

Lilly put out her hand to draw Tina down beside her, but she turned away from the touch. Lilly's hand remained poised, for an instant. Then she withdrew it, saying, "Don't shrink away from me, Tina. I've done nothing wrong. I only did what was necessary, and right." Tina turned to stare at her incredulously.

Lilly exclaimed pettishly, "Oh, how can I talk to you when you loom over me so? Do find a chair and sit down." Tina obeyed her.

Lilly addressed an imaginary bystander. "Now why should I be accountable, of all people, to Tina?" She smiled at her own question. "I'm not, of course. I don't have to explain anything to you, do I?" Lilly looked at Tina with reproach. "I do wish you didn't have that way of constantly staring at one with so much imploring inquiry. It borders on bad manners; it's not the sort of habit I should permit my children to fall into." Tina, amazed at this attack, was unable to reply. Lilly continued. "But then, I can't afford to set up a quarrel with you, can I? I do want you to stay on here and close things up. Someone has to get Goddard and the girls back to school." Lilly was not prepared for Tina's continued silence. She ran her fingers through her as yet uncombed hair impatiently. "Oh, very well. Perhaps I ought to explain. Anyway, you already know the 'worst,' don't you?"

Lilly searched about in her mind for a beginning. As she collected her thoughts she acknowledged, "There is a certain relief in confession, after all. It hardly matters whether or not you agree with me, and yet I may as well tell it all to you. I can't tell everything, even to Findlay. Why not to you? You've always been avid to know the reasons why we do the things we do, haven't you? Like an anthropologist studying the natives. Only here, I suppose you find it a little more difficult being almost a part of the tribe. Very well then, let me begin, oh, not at the beginning, but a long time ago.

"When I was your age, I was in love, I thought. Not with anyone you know. I'd met him at school. He was from Iowa. Nobody anyone knew, really, and I was finally brought to realize that it would never do. They were right—I wasn't meant to share his sort of life and if we'd married we would both have been unhappy. Instead, I finished school, and then drifted for a while. In a few years, I married your father. But, although our marriage was suitable in every way, and I soon had my children, Skippy was never really there with me. I don't think either of us was miserable, we liked each other and understood each other. There just wasn't any real contact between us. So, you see, after he'd died and I was a widow, I'd already had two rather unsatisfactory relationships with men. I hadn't been a widow long, and I was only twenty-six when Findlay Hemmingway and I began to go out together. You'll find it hard to understand how relieved and even grateful I was that he wanted to marry me. He was a good deal older but he had never married. He belonged to my world, and I could respect him. He seemed to be strong and certain, compared to Skippy, and he was sure he wanted me. He never tried to become a father to my children, but he was glad, rather than the contrary, that I had children. Because he wanted a family of his own, of course. He'd looked around for a long time, and he'd decided that I'd be an ideal wife for him, and I was more than flattered, I was thrilled, because I agreed with him. When we were married, I finally felt that my life had succeeded and I was secure. My husband adored me and it was very pleasant to be adored and we were happy. But a few years passed, and we weren't quite so happy any more. Marriage, when all is said and done, is a contract, but I hadn't lived up to my part of our bargain, because I hadn't given him a child. And Findlay was nearing fifty then, and he wanted his name to continue, he wanted a son.

"I think the worst part of it, for him, was the fact that I'd already shown I was capable of having children— there were Mimsi and Goddard, who had come so easily when Skippy had never even cared particularly. For a while I hoped, anyway, that there might be something that had gone wrong with me, and I went to doctors and took all the tests, but without any result. That wasn't to say that it wasn't my fault, they just didn't know. When they don't find anything wrong, it still doesn't mean everything is right. Of course, it might have been Findlay's fault. That was possible, but it might also be that there was some incompatibility between us. And the last thing I could have done was to suggest to Findlay that he was incapable in any way. I think it might be even worse for a man than for a woman to think that he was at fault, particularly a man like Findlay, who prides himself on his strength and his superiority."

Lilly paused, and gazed for a moment at her hands, tanned and unadorned save for the single square emerald she wore on her left hand, with her wedding ring. She twisted the stone without looking at it. Then her voice began again. "Things weren't happy for us any more and Findlay began to keep away from me. He traveled a lot —he always had—but one summer he didn't ask me to make the trip with him. Instead, I brought my children back to the island, and then I decided to do something. I had to. Of course, I was careful. Any woman would be. I don't just mean that I was discreet. I wanted the best father I could find for the child I hoped I'd have, someone who'd give me a child I could be proud of. And finally I decided on Charles Corbin. It wasn't very hard after that."

Reflexively, Lilly glanced across at her reflection in the mirror; the image she saw seemed reassuring to her. "I didn't ask him to fall in love with me, I never wanted or expected that. I just wanted the child. And, of course, it worked, and I had Finny. I knew I had done the right thing when Findlay held him up in chapel after the christening. He had his son and we were happy again. In fact, his world began to revolve around Finny. Well, that was fine. Findlay was never unkind to my children, you understand, he was just uninterested in them. For a while I don't even think he was very interested in me, either; it was all Finny. And of course Finny was an engaging little blond baby, not much different from my other babies, or from any other child on the island.

"But, he began to grow up. He's a handsome little boy, don't you think? But he doesn't resemble me and, of course, he's nothing at all like Findlay. Still, I don't think Findlay ever would have had a question, if it hadn't been that Charles continued to fancy himself in love with me. Every summer on the island Findlay saw us together, and finally, I suppose, he saw Charles and Finny in one glance, and he began to be suspicious. I begged Charles to keep away from me, but there was always a party or a dance where we'd be bound to exchange greetings, and I could see Findlay looking at us, and wondering. Finally, I suppose, he made up his own mind as to the truth. He never said anything to me; there was nothing to confront me with. After all, I'd never been in love with Charles and our affair had concluded abruptly as soon as I'd discovered I'd conceived. But, he began to avoid Finny, too. That hurt. It hurt me, but it was hurting Finny more. The change in his father's behavior toward him was so marked. It made him very unhappy." Again Lilly played with her ring before looking up at Tina.

"Findlay and I began to have quarrels. Not over anything significant, just over little meaningless things. We never mentioned what we were really arguing about. When Findlay announced this spring that he was taking an extended tour of Africa on behalf of his foundation, I was relieved. It would be better to have him far away than living with us on the terms we'd been on. When he went he more or less said that he didn't expect to be coming back to me." She paused, for a long time. "He told me he was leaving. We had a scene. He said he knew I'd been unfaithful to him, he supposed that I was always having affairs behind his back; he said that he'd been wrong to think he could trust a woman so much younger than he. He was abusive and unfair. I couldn't talk to him; I could never have made him understand. He'd been so proud of his son; I suppose that was why he was so wild with rage."

Tina had listened in silence; it was an effort to try to comprehend. Lilly's charge stung. It was true, she had been viewing Lilly and her crowd like a puzzle set out for her edification, but worse, she had been living with them for weeks, known Lilly for years, and had had no inkling of the realities. Yet, without digesting any of what Lilly had told her, she was impelled to ask, "How can you be going back with him, you and Finny, now that he knows the truth?"

Lilly looked at her almost with amusement at her perplexity. "So that's what you can't cope with? You think there should be a great dramatic crisis now, endless recriminations, Finny disowned, due punishment inflicted on me, on us all. But, Tina, what a disappointment for you. It's all going to be all right, because now Findlay understands. He understands that I was right. We have Finny; that's what really matters."

Lilly's look challenged Tina to contradict her. Tina had no wish to do so. She was far from feeling the disappointment which Lilly had imputed to her. She had formed no judgment at all. She was more intimidated than enthralled at having been made privy to Lilly's secrets. She had never believed that real people, people she knew, could become embroiled in such events. She was relieved that Lilly had ceased her confessions, ceased burdening her with the confidences she seemed to enjoy rather than fear to place in Tina's hands. But even this sense of relief was not proof against her besetting need to probe the inherent improbability in Lilly's recitation. She had to ask one question: "How did you persuade your husband that what you did was right?"

Lilly gave Tina a careful glance of reappraisal. "Then it's not my morals but my methods that you're interested in. You've surprised me, Tina. And yet, you're right. While Findlay was away, I thought I might never be able to convince him that I was right. It seemed quite desperate. But when he came back from Africa, he was already persuaded. It was something he saw, he experienced on his trip, that made the truth acceptable to him. He told me about it. Through part of Africa, in Chad and the Sudan, they're having the most awful drought. Whole families and tribes are starving, and they're trekking south looking for food and new lands they can settle on. Findlay was traveling through the poorest, most backward of these areas, in the border area between Sudan and Uganda, surveying the effects of the drought on wildlife conditions. His party fell in with some of these refugees who'd been moving for more than a year, traveling down from the Sudan. There were very few children left alive with them, and those there were were emaciated and sickly. The night they camped nearby a child died, and in the morning, when he was buried, his guide told Findlay the story. He had been the last child of a large number; he had been the last son. The father was pointed out, an old, old man. Findlay was amazed at the resignation with which he bore his grief. The guide explained that the tribe expected to reach new lands where they had been promised resettlement, and this aged man had faith that he would have many more sons, and his tribe would endure. Of course, Findlay was incredulous. The old man looked to be about to die himself. But it was explained. The old man had two young wives, and he could trust them to provide him with more children, even in his old age. While there were still young men in the tribe, his wives would see to it that they would bear him more sons, and his line would not die."

Lilly's voice trailed off. Tina put her hand over her eyes. She would probe no further; whether or not this narrative were true and had worked a transformation, Lilly and Findlay Hemmingway were content with it. "Please, Lilly," Tina asked. "Don't say any more. I don't have to understand. I don't want to know. It's not my concern, nor anyone else's. I certainly won't talk about it; it's the last thing I'd do. But you must know that."

Lilly was satisfied. "And you will stay on here after I've left. You'll cope."

Tina assented numbly to Lilly's request, as always.

The door was flung open and Findlay Hemmingway strode into the cluttered room. Effortlessly he ignored Tina and addressed his wife. "Lilly, there was a most unpleasant young woman downstairs. She was waiting to see one of us, so I saw her." He paused for breath.

Lilly did not quite understand; Tina did. She exclaimed, "Maria. I'd forgotten about Maria."

"Maria?" Lilly was alarmed. "What did she want here?"

"Money," Hemmingway stated baldly. He was indignant. "A servant and she had the effrontery to come here to demand money."

Lilly sat down heavily. Her husband continued, oblivious to her reaction. "I sent her off in a hurry!" He said to Lilly, critically, "How in the world did you come to hire such a person? I thought I could absolutely rely on your judgment in servants."

Lilly broke into helpless laughter. After all this, Findlay had dispatched the baleful Maria with a few choice words. Tina could not help but observe the irony of the situation; Hemmingway's indignation had been reserved for Lilly's apparent poor choice of hired help. Findlay Hemmingway eyed his wife incredulously, but his mood was magnanimous. "Well, I fail to see the joke, but very well, have your laugh."

Lilly's merriment subsided. "And you didn't even ask her what it was she expected to blackmail us about?"

Findlay drew himself up, outraged. "Certainly not. A servant's gossip could not be of the slightest interest to me."

Lilly stared up at him admiringly.

Chapter 16

To the general relief of those who were remaining, the Hemmingways had departed serenely. Mimsi was delighted that whatever rift had developed in her mother's marriage had been mended. Her cousins were pleased for her sake; the prospect of divorcing parents was never a cheerful one. Goddard was not vocal as to his sentiments, but the loss of Lilly's presence did not appear to be detrimental to his happiness. Tina was as glad as Mimsi to see their amicable departure, but she, unlike the others who had been permitted the bliss of ignorance, had an alloy to her pleasure. She could not help pondering at length over Lilly's own account of her conduct and motives. Had she been right? Not according to any conventional standards, but hadn't the results justified her? There was Finny, who would not otherwise have existed, and Lilly and Findlay had faced the truth and were quite reconciled. Who, then, had been hurt? Only Charles, perhaps. Lilly had neither contemplated nor cared for that. She had meant only to use him, as she had assumed he would be utilizing her. That Charles had professed himself still to care for her, to have become obsessed with what was no longer a profitable relationship for Lilly, seemed to be little more than an unfortunate accident.

What would Charles do now? Tina wondered. Had Lilly even bothered to inform him of the change in her own life before departing for Africa? And of what concern was any of this now, to Tina? In a few more days she would supervise the closing of the house. Mrs. Chambers and Hodges would do the actual work, assisted by Fentiman. Then, all packed, they would be driven to the city where Tina could dispatch the girls and Goddard back to their respective boarding schools. Her task was really over and she doubted if she would ever again be summoned to Mallard Cottage. She would be twenty-one during the year. All legal ties to this family would then be severed, and the Hemmingways would hardly welcome in future a girl who was already far too intimate with their personal affairs. Although Tina told herself that these were the truths of her situation, she was unable to shake off the feelings of involvement and responsibility which the past summer had imposed upon her. As often as she tried to turn her thoughts forward, to her return to the city and to her mother, to the resumption, for a time at least, of her studies, they strayed defiantly to the tumultuous events of the recent and not so recent past.

With Lilly gone, the oppressive requirement that she ride herd on the girls had been lifted from her. They were happy enough with their own friends, making their farewells at the last flings which had been planned to close the season on the island, and had little further need of her. She could assume that Goddard had his own resources. She certainly saw little of him, but that had been the pattern of the summer and had caused no comment. Of all the children, Goddard came in for the least family notice. He appeared content, or resigned, to this position. Tina saw no reason to make an attempt to depart from the even tenor of their ways during these last days. In any event, she was certain that his self-sufficiency would be proof against any belated effort she might make to establish some point of contact with her half-brother.

The junior set would have a barbeque at the beach club and an informal dance on Sunday night. Their seniors would attend the final big dance of the season at the golf club. The Monday of Labor Day itself would see endless and overlapping private farewell parties before the departures began. Tina found herself at loose ends. With no friends of her own to take leave of, and no call of duty to require her presence at any of these festivities, she foresaw for herself a quiet time, spent on the beach in the daytime and in her room with a book at night, while she recovered her equilibrium and prepared to re-enter her own life.

It was with surprise and reluctance that she received a call from Helen Corbin asking her to join their party up at Hill House on Labor Day. Tina shrank from attending a cocktail party of near strangers, but worse, she dreaded the inevitable confrontations which acceptance of this invitation would bring. She wanted to avoid seeing Charles. After their last encounter and Lilly's subsequent disclosure, she did not know how she could face him. She had not heard from Tony Corbin after their brief interlude at the Yacht Club. That day now seemed far away. She was sure that he had regretted the impulse which had led him to seek her out. The memory of their approach to friendship must surely have been blotted out by her abrupt insistence on leaving the Yacht Club. He had been very angry indeed. Tina concluded she had run away once too often for him. She did not expect that he would try again. She could foresee nothing but embarrassment for her if she appeared at his parents' party. Politely, but not regretfully, she made her excuses. She would be busy; it was their last day on the island; Lilly had left her in charge of closing up; she didn't think she could possibly accept. She hoped Mrs. Corbin would understand. But Helen Corbin, while acquiescing in her refusal, appeared determined to have a last talk with Tina. "Then, perhaps, you can join me for lunch today? Now, don't tell me you won't be eating anyway. You can't be that busy. After all, what are the servants there for? Come up and see me for lunch. We'll be quite alone, and just have a little conversation. Shall we say one?" Tina consented; the assurance that their meal would be quite private had swayed her. But she wondered at the older woman's anxiety to secure her company.

Tina changed into a shirtdress. Somehow, she didn't think she could go to luncheon with Mrs. Corbin, no matter how informally, in denim pants and bare feet.

Surveying herself in the mirror of the yellow room, she realized how much the summer had changed her. It was not only that the tan she had acquired was becoming, nor that the new look produced by her cousins deft ministrations—even as adapted and modified by Tina to suit the demands of everyday existence—had changed her previously plain appearance to something more arresting. There was a difference in her stance, in her air of greater assurance. Not even to herself did she still resemble the shy, lanky, post-adolescent who had duly arrived at Mallard Cottage in answer to Lilly's peremptory summons. Internally, she wondered if she wasn't actually unchanged, but externally she looked self-confident as she descended to the car and was driven to keep her luncheon engagement.

As Helen Corbin had stated, they were alone. Her hostess proffered no explanations as to the absence of her husband and sons, but led Tina onto the terrace upon which they had previously conversed, where a luncheon table for two had been set in the shade of a garden umbrella.

As Helen Corbin led their conversation, Tina had to

remind herself that most of what had transpired in the last week was unknown to her hostess, and had better remain so. She would have to guard her tongue, for Mrs. Corbin had shown herself to be astute, for example, in judging from Tina's refusal of the invitation to the party that she might be more willing to join her in a tête-à-tête. Not that there was any obvious attempt to pump Tina. But their talk led among dangerous topics. Helen Corbin commented quite naturally on Findlay Hemmingway's sudden arrival, followed so closely by the three Hemmingways' abrupt departure. In the scale of island gossip, an event so unexpected and inexplicable must indeed have been a godsend, Tina had to remind herself. Mention of it to her was only to be expected. Mrs. Corbin said, "Not that I'm surprised at all at any of Findlay Hemmingway's sudden starts. I've known him forever, you see. Always given to snap decisions, and once made, not lightly departed from. Take the way he decided to marry Lilly when she was widowed. Once he'd made up his mind, it was all over but the ceremony. I suppose he took it into his head that she belonged with him traipsing through Africa, though what comfort he expects to find in dragging an elegant creature like Lilly and their little boy through the deserts and jungles is more than I can understand. No use asking you how he prevailed on Lilly to go. She's got determination of her own, but Hemmingway's her master." She added, "Good thing, too. That's the way it should be." Tina found, gratefully, that she was only called upon to provide assent to her hostess's judgments on the state of facts known to her.

But with their dessert and iced tea, Tina found herself again challenged as Helen Corbin asked her, "I suppose you're wondering why I was so anxious to see you. Well, I'll be blunt; I expect you've noticed by now that I speak my mind. I like you. You're young, I suppose, but you're a serious, sensible sort of girl. You're attractive and you've the right background. When all is said and done, you're well-connected. You are a Mallard." Tina couldn't help thinking to herself with amusement that she wondered if Mrs. Corbin would consider that to be a recommendation if she knew everything about the Mallards and their connections that she herself did. "Not that I mean to say that that's a prime consideration any more. But it helps, one can't deny that." Tina waited, unsuspiciously. Was Mrs. Corbin about to offer her a position or a recommendation for some job? She'd be needing one, soon enough, and if so, it was very thoughtful of her. "You may be wondering what I'm leading up to. I hope not, I hope you know." She paused to look enquiringly at Tina. Tina shook her head. "Then I suppose I'll have to come out with it." Helen Corbin gathered her forces of persuasion before plunging ahead. "Charles is thirty. He ought to marry. Don't say it's no concern of mine, because it is. He's had years to look around, and dozens of girls would have been glad to have him. You can't deny that. But he hasn't made a move. Well, it's time to give him a push. You like him; it would be amazing if you didn't. And I have more than a suspicion that he thinks you're rather special. Change your mind and come to my party on Monday. When we're back in the city, I'll see that you join us for the theater, for dinner, that you're together frequently. Once you're brought together, it won't be long before the penny will drop. Charles needs a wife and he'll soon realize that you would suit him perfectly." Tina sat in bewildered silence, totally at a loss as to how even to begin to reply. Helen Corbin, managing a smile, went on. "Well, well, I suppose I have taken you by surprise after all. You look quite dumbfounded."

Tina nodded. "Yes, I am surprised. Awfully."

"Well, you needn't be. You can tell me I'm a meddlesome old woman, but you can't say my plan doesn't have merit. You couldn't do better for yourself, admit that. I'm just trying to give things a push in the right direction. Sometimes that's all that's needed."

"But Charles," Tina interrupted, "why should you think that he would fall in love with me?"

"Why not?" Helen Corbin challenged. "When the time comes, he's going to ask some girl he knows. I'd just as soon not leave it all to chance; I'd rather it was you."

Tina shook her head in disbelief. Could it be that marriages were still—not quite "arranged"—but suggested, in this way? "Mrs. Corbin, what you've said is very flattering to me, I realize that, but I can't believe that propinquity is all that's needed."

"Can't you? Look at some of the marriages around you. It's the only explanation in most cases." Tina continued to appear confused, and Helen Corbin placed her own interpretation on this evidence. "Well, well, you're still young and it's understandable to me that you should be a bit shy. You needn't say anything or commit yourself. Just think it over. I'll expect you to come on Monday, then, shall I?"

Tina felt compelled to say, "I still don't know. I really can't say now."

"Think it over," Mrs. Corbin repeated. Then, changing the subject, "What do you think of my hydrangeas? A little spindly and overgrown, don't you agree? I'll give orders to have them well pruned back this spring. We may lose the blossom next summer, but it will be worth it in years to come."

"I'm sure you're right," Tina agreed, not knowing if this gardening wisdom was sound or not. And she continued to bear a most abstracted part in the conversation until Fentiman finally called for her.

Could his mother possibly be right? Was it likely that Charles would fall in love with her on the delayed rebound, as it were, now that Lilly had decamped? This latter factor could not have played a part in his mother's calculations, but Tina could not dismiss it from her thoughts. If someday, say in six months, after he'd gotten used to her company and she to his, Charles Corbin should ask her to be his wife, would she be willing? His mother clearly anticipated no such hesitation on Tina's part. She obviously considered that any girl whom Charles finally decided to marry would be fortunate indeed. And certainly she had reason. There was no one else so handsome, so kind, so charming, or, of course, so well-bred, well-connected, and wealthy. Why then was she not overwhelmed with joy at the prospect? His mother's interference was undoubtedly well meant. She shouldn't allow the feeling of conniving at a bargain that their talk had engendered in her to weigh against Charles, who was obviously unaware of his mother's role. Wouldn't she be foolish in refusing to become better acquainted with him, knowing as she did that the obstacle to his falling in love with someone else had now been removed by Lilly's departure? And, if he were to marry, wasn't it likely that as his mother predicted his choice would then fall on her? Why should she hesitate? She wasn't even committing herself by agreeing to Helen Corbin's proposal simply to join them on any number of social occasions, a prospect which, alone, ought to have been attractive to her. Why not?

Chapter 17

Hardly noticing what she was doing, Tina saw the girls off to their beach party, and returned to her room and book, which lay long unopened on her lap as she remained sunk in her reverie. The days were already beginning to grow shorter, and it was the fact that she was sitting in semi-darkness that roused Tina at last. As she crossed to the lamp to snap on the light, the realization suddenly came to her that while she had seen the girls at dinner before waving goodbye to them as they left for the beach club, Goddard had neither appeared nor left any message as to his whereabouts.

Quickly Tina checked his room, but it was deserted. A rapid search through the rest of the house revealed only bleak emptiness, emphasized by the signs that packing up had already begun. Where could Goddard be? Could he have brought himself to attend the beach party and dance? Unlikely, but possible. Tina clutched at this straw with relief. For if he wasn't at the party, where was he? She hadn't seen him since breakfast—no, wait, he'd breakfasted before the rest of them today. He'd mentioned that this would be his last big day; after Labor

Day his boat would have to be taken out of the water and stored, and he'd planned to spend Labor Day itself bringing the boat up to the yard.

Tina telephoned the beach club. When Mimsi finally was brought to the phone, she had no idea of her brother's whereabouts and was not inclined to interrupt her own pursuits to hunt for him. At Tina's urging, she agreed at least to take a quick look around with Brooke and Leigh, but when she returned to the telephone her report was negative. "And we did truly look, Tina, because whatever I may have said, when I started thinking I realized that it is strange that he's not at home. But he isn't here. We even asked some of these younger creeps but no one's seen him. Actually he doesn't hang around with anyone I know; I doubt if he would be visiting anywhere. Still, there's nothing to take on about. He's probably safe and out in his boat. Mother never worried about him when she knew he was out sailing, you know."

"You don't mean he could still be out on the boat?" Tina asked tensely.

"Well," Mimsi answered doubtfully, "you know, he could be. There's plenty of moonlight and it's quite calm, so he'll be all right if he is. Besides, where else *could* he be?"

Tina had no ready answer. But as she hung up the instrument, she knew that her first step must be to see whether his boat had returned. She found Fentiman relaxing in the servants' dining hall with Mrs. Chambers, the cook, over a couple of bottles of beer, and without pausing even to comb her hair Tina had the car brought around, and was driven to the Yacht Club. The clubhouse was darkened and locked. It was only then that Tina realized that she was unable to tell where to look for Goddard's boat; she didn't know where it should be moored, and peering into the moonlit night at the gentle waves in the harbor, she was unable to make out which, if any, of the silhouetted shapes rocking to and fro at their moorings might be Goddard's Bullseye. She had to find Tony Corbin.

Tina dashed across the street to the still brightly lit coffee shop to use their telephone. The seats at the fountain were occupied by several of the casual tourists who might be expected to land on the island for a big weekend, although they would not be attending any of the planned festivities which marked the in-group's farewell to the season. Max, the owner, was serving these few visitors, and he agreed to let her use his telephone. Tina dialed the Corbins' number rapidly, relieved that she had been able to bring it to mind without losing time to consult a directory. The phone rang forever it seemed, but finally it was answered.

"This is Tina Mallard. Is Tony there? May I please speak with him?"

"I'm speaking," Tony answered matter-of-factly.

"Oh, thank goodness. I was afraid you might be at the golf club dance. Tony, please, meet me at the Yacht Club, right away."

"Hold on, what is this about, my girl? You sound all in a panic."

"It's Goddard. I suddenly realized—I don't know where he is. I haven't seen him all day. Maybe he still has his boat out; maybe he's in trouble. Only I can't tell. I don't know one boat from the other, especially in the dark. Oh, Tony, please come and help me," Tina pleaded frantically.

"Get a grip on yourself. I'll be right there," and he hung up.

Calmer now, Tina retraced her steps to the gangplank leading to the Yacht Club to await Tony's arrival. She sent Fentiman home, with an injunction to phone her immediately at the Yacht Club should Goddard turn up, or a message from him arrive. Then, pacing back and forth, rubbing her icy hands together, she waited impatiently for the few minutes it took before Tony's battered gray Volkswagen chugged down the street and drew up next to her. Tony alighted and, preceding her up the gangplank, opened the locked door to the Yacht Club and flipped on the lights.

"Now, then, what is all this?" he repeated.

"Don't keep saying that," Tina replied. "I've told you. Goddard isn't home. He's been gone all day. When I suddenly realized that it was night time and he still hadn't turned up I got panicky. Now will you please tell me whether or not his boat is tied up or docked, or whatever you call it?"

"Do you mean that a fourteen-year-old kid left in your charge has been missing since morning and you're just waking up to the fact?"

"Don't you start accusing me of carelessness. I assure you you couldn't say anything worse to me than I've already told myself. But you see, Lilly left him on such a free rein, and never seemed to worry about him, and nothing ever happened. I could hardly insist that he be housebound these last few days with me, could I? Besides, why are you blowing up at me? It's not your place to criticize me, Tony Corbin."

"Only for the very good reason that I'm a little worried myself. I know he took his boat out early this morning. I didn't see him at the docks myself but it was taken out. Probably I should have checked to see that he'd moored before I left. I just assumed he'd come in. He's such a good sailor, and the ocean's so calm, that I never gave him a thought either."

"Do you mean that you're worried too? But you just said that you trusted him and, with the weather so good, what could have happened?"

"Listen, Tina. It's not likely that there's anything wrong, but use your head. A kid alone in a boat could have had any of a number of accidents, from stupidly letting himself get hit in the head by the boom when he jibbed, to being run down by some idiot in a stinkpot out for a Sunday thrill ride. We won't know anything until I check." Walking past her, he stooped to open a locker and pull out a pair of oars and oarlocks, which he shouldered.

"What are you doing now?" Tina exclaimed in frustration. "Is this a time to go rowing?"

"Did you think I could check his mooring from here? This weekend, of all times, the launch has broken down. I don't know why a club like this can't have more than one launch, but the trustees who run it dread anything that smacks of ostentation. Two launches might be convenient, but a little too showy. So, I've got to row out and look around. Do you want to come along? No, wait— On second thought, if he's not in, you'd better stay here. Then, if I signal you, you can call the Coast Guard and alert them to look out for him."

"But how will I know? What would I say?" Tina wailed.

Tony explained patiently: "If you see me signal with my flashlight—three long flashes, one after the other, get on the phone. Here's a dime. The number is posted right on the wall. Tell them to start a search. Describe the boat, it's a Herreshoff Bullseye. They'll know what to do." Tony gripped her shoulder with his free hand. "And hang loose. Nothing will have happened to him. Chances are we'll find his boat at the mooring and then when we catch up with him we can take turns kicking his butt for being an irresponsible little fool and making us both worry. Okay?"

Tina smiled back at him, but her feeble attempt was marred by the watery haze which obscured her vision of him. Swearing to himself, Tony turned, walked out to the end of the dock, and dropped lightly into the boat tied up there. He pushed off with one oar and after a few seconds was lost both to sight and hearing. Tina strained her eyes to make out a glimpse of his progress and finally caught sight of him as he rowed across the path the moon laid down across the waters. Then he vanished again. She stood frozen at the end of the dock, scanning the wavelet-marked harbor afraid to move for fear of missing Tony's signal, and even more afraid that it would come. Again and again she thought she could make out the faint sound of oars, that it must be Tony returning to tell her that he'd found the boat, but each hope turned out to be false. It seemed to Tina that he had had time to fine-comb the harbor, and still the rowboat had not returned.

Finally, when she found herself wishing for a cigarette, although she had rarely smoked one in her life, she saw the lights. The boat was missing. Something had happened to Goddard.

Tina ran for the telephone, struggled to make sure of the numbers, and dialed. The Coast Guard station was located on the mainland, she knew, not many miles east of the island. Perhaps they would already have found him, she hoped. Her report was received unemotionally, but not unsympathetically. Goddard was alone in his Bullseye; he had set out at sometime between eight and nine that morning. He was said to be an experienced sailor, but he was only fourteen. She had no idea of what course he planned to set. She was promised that they would be on the alert for any such craft. But Tina felt this was small assurance. After she replaced the receiver she began to sob convulsively. She was in tears when Tony walked in to replace the oars.

"Oh, Tony," she wailed. "Tony, are you sure? What took you so long?"

"It took me so long because *now* I am sure," he answered grimly. "His boat wasn't where it should be, but I had to check to see that it hadn't slipped its mooring and drifted in toward the inlet. Then, we have several other boats of the same class at the club; I wanted to check on each of them to make sure that there wasn't any confusion. I wanted to be positive before I signaled. You called the Coast Guard?" Tina nodded. "Well, then, take my handkerchief if you haven't got one and blow your nose. Don't fall to pieces on me. He's not lost yet."

"I'm sorry," she apologized. "I won't let go again, I promise you. But Tony, must we just sit here and wait to hear from the Coast Guard? Isn't there anything else that we can do?"

"Hush up a minute. Let me think."

Tina clasped her hands in her lap and dutifully waited. Finally, he smiled down at her as she sat silently on the locker gazing up at him expectantly.

"Did he ever say anything to you, Tina, anything at all, about where he might be planning to go today?"

Tina retained her self-control with effort. In an anguished voice she replied, "Oh, Tony, that's what makes it so awful. Goddard never confided in anyone. The others seemed to accept it, so I did. Lilly's been too preoccupied with her own concerns, the girls had each other, and Finny was too young. Goddard didn't even have a best friend. He came and went all summer like a boarder. At first I thought that he was reticent with me in particular, but I see now that it was the same thing with his own sister. They're away at different schools all winter; they hardly know each other either. It's not right that a boy be left to himself that much, is it? There was bound to be trouble. I should have done something, made some effort."

"Tina. Stop wallowing in guilt. You're hardly to blame if Goddard's gotten into difficulty out sailing. As for the rest of it, I can't imagine any healthy fourteen-year-old boy being particularly communicative with his own family. Besides, whatever you might have done, these recriminations aren't of the least use right now. Just stick to facts, and see if there isn't any little thing you can remember."

Tina tried. "He was excited about today. It was his last

time out in the boat until next summer. I think he was looking forward to doing something special—at least, it was special to him. But I know nothing about sailing. I've never even been out in a boat." She paused as she caught his look of amazement, then continued. "So you see, he wouldn't have discussed it with me."

Tony nodded. "Then have the car pick up the girls from the beach club and bring them here. Call Mimsi and ask her to bring along any of the boys whom he might have talked to, anyone who's crewed for him in a race, anyone about his own age. You never can tell, they might know something."

"But if he was going to try something new, wouldn't he have talked it over with you first, Tony?" she asked.

"That very much depends on what he was up to. If he had some feat of daring in mind, I can guess that he'd want to do it first, and then come back and astonish me with it. He'd want to do it all by himself. On the other hand, if he was up to something else, then he certainly wouldn't have discussed it with me."

"What else? What can you mean?" Tina implored.

"There are a few suspicions lurking in my mind. A solitary boy of Goddard's age would be very susceptible to the temptation of trying to prove his daring in other ways too."

"Temptation? Here, on the island? What temptation?"

"Especially here on the island, where we do what we please and set our own standards and the only thing that's unforgivable is creating a scandal about it." He saw her worried expression as she weighed the possibilities. "Look, don't imagine the worst. All we need to do right now is get an idea of where he was heading so that the Coast Guard will have a chance of picking him up."

"But, how far could he have gone?" Tina enquired anxiously.

"It all depends. With a good breeze blowing, and depending on his course, he might have made as much as eighty miles, you know."

"Eighty miles," Tina repeated incredulously.

"Oh, that's assuming he had a good run with the tide and the wind with him all the way. I doubt if he was setting that sort of course. For one thing, that's sailing steadily before the wind and with the tide. He would have had to allow time for tacking, and for coming about and getting back to the island. He really can't have gone that far. Even if he was out to demonstrate his sailing prowess, there are only a few courses that would have presented him with the challenge of pulling off something spectacular on his last day."

"Go on," Tina breathed.

"He might have headed out on a course to intersect the end of the Cape and planned to turn and come back in the same day—but that's a pretty stiff sail; he might have kept on south once he was out of the harbor, heading for Rocky Point; or he might have tried to make it out to the old lighthouse off the rocks at the end of the channel. I don't know which he'd aim at. And with a wide open field, there's just that much less chance of locating him. But if he mentioned to anyone which way he was heading, it won't be hard to find him when the sun rises and before a lot of other boats set out for a Labor Day sail." Tina understood.

Calmly, she called the cottage directing Fentiman to go to the beach club immediately. Still calmly, she spoke again to Mimsi on the telephone. Mimsi now seemed to grasp that the situation could be serious and promised to bring Brooke and Leigh, and anyone else who might be at all helpful. It wasn't long before their subdued party arrived. Mimsi led the way, followed by her cousins, and by two youths who were vaguely familiar to Tina. Tony, at least, seemed to be well acquainted with them.

The girls gave every sign of intensive self-searching

when Tony had explained the problem to them, but
without result. Brooke explained, "He never talked to
us, either, Tina. I guess we treated him too much like a
kid. I mean, even if he was just a year younger than me,
at fourteen a boy's just not very interesting, is he?"

Mimsi gulped. "I know he's my own brother. But he
was so independent. Oh, dear—I mean *is.*" She burst
into tears.

Tony jerked his head at Tina. "Take them home, will
you. There's no point in letting them have mass hysterics
here."

Tina resisted his request. "Fentiman can drive them
back. I want to stay here with you."

Tony drew her aside. "Don't argue. I think I'll do
better talking to the boys alone."

Tina thrust her chin up at him. "Okay, but *I'm* coming
back. I want to wait here, with you."

"Just be a good girl and take them away. I'll still be
here if you decide to return, don't worry." Then, as they
left in a gale of sobs, with Tina's arm resting comfort-
ingly around her small half-sister's shoulders, he turned
to the two boys.

"Now you didn't come up from the beach club just out
of curiosity, did you guys? I have my suspicions as to
what's been going on, and I'm sure you know . . ." She
heard Tony say, as they passed out of hearing.

Once at the cottage, Tina found more on her hands
than she had anticipated. The three girls alternated in
giving way to despair and she finally had to wake Mrs.
Chambers, to ask her to fix a pot of cocoa for them, and
keep an eye on them until she returned. Deciding to
leave Fentiman at the cottage, Tina hopped on a bicycle
and pedaled furiously back to the Yacht Club, where she
found Tony, quite alone.

In answer to her anxious look of enquiry, he shook his
head. "No, still no word from the Coast Guard. I doubt

if they'd be able to pick him up before sunrise."

"But didn't the boys have anything to say, after all?" asked Tina.

"Well, they did and they didn't," he replied. "It rather seems that Goddard had planned a very special last outing. They don't know where he was heading. He hadn't confided in them to that extent. Goddard didn't have any real buddies. But these boys have crewed for him in some races, and they did talk occasionally. Mark, at least, had the impression that Goddard's venture was not going to be solitary. He says he saw him taking a girl out to the Bullseye this morning. And Graham says that Goddard had hinted as much. It seems yesterday they were giving him some chaff about his apparent lack of success with Maria compared to all the fun they'd been having, and Goddard let it be known that he was planning to finish his summer off in high style."

Tina looked perplexed. "You can't mean that he's taken Maria with him?"

"I don't suppose you ever actually suggested to Lilly that she increase Goddard's pocket money, did you?" Tony asked. Tina dropped her eyes before his amused gaze. "Well, I guess he had formulated his own ideas as to how he was going to prove that he was a man."

"But surely you're joking. It can't be possible," Tina asserted. She continued with less assurance. "Although I must admit that Maria certainly is a strange girl. She as much as told me one day that she was out for money, however she could get it; she seemed to equate it with success. Then, she turned up at the cottage while Findlay Hemmingway was there, and tried to get money out of him. He hustled her out in short order."

"What was she trying to sell him? Herself?"

Tina had to laugh. "Really! In the sun room at Mallard Cottage at eleven in the morning? No, there was some implication that she wanted to be paid not to talk."

"She tried to blackmail Findlay Hemmingway?" This

time it was Tony who laughed. "The last man in the world to submit, I'd guess. Not only does he set his own standards, he's so far above every one in his own estimation that he wouldn't even care about their gossip. But what deep dark family secret can she hold in her hot little hands?"

Tina fell silent. She was never going to discuss this subject, especially not with Tony Corbin. She evaded answering by saying, "I suppose every family has some skeleton more or less securely locked away in a cupboard."

Taking the hint, Tony did not press the point. "Let's leave it that Maria is, as you said, an odd girl. She may even be more unusually enterprising than I had thought. There seems to be another explanation, in addition to the most obvious one, for her sensational popularity among the kids on the island this summer. But what's more immediate cause for concern is that, whatever her attractions, she's not an ideal sailing companion for a kid like Goddard."

"But at least he's not all by himself. What was frightening me was the thought that he might be injured, with no one to help him."

"That *is* a point of view. On the other hand, I'd feel much better if I knew he'd gone out alone. Not only will he be trying to show off if she's on board, but I don't imagine that she's anything of a sailor. An untrained crew can be worse than no one at all. No, I'm afraid that if we find him"—seeing Tina's expression he rapidly corrected himself——"I mean when, we'll find out that she's been the cause of the trouble."

Tina looked frightened. "You said *if.* Oh, Tony. Isn't there anything we can do?"

Tony looked thoughtful. "Of course, if Maria's along, I can't believe he set out to break any sailing records, if you see what I mean. That indicates he wouldn't have been planning to go so far out." Suddenly, he shot her a wicked grin. "I'll bet I know where he headed."

Tina felt hopeful. "Have you really thought of something, Tony?"

"Well, it's the usual place, but I don't know why they wouldn't have made it back long before dark."

"Where would he go? What do you mean?" Tina asked.

"You see, my dear, there's a little island, about five miles out. It's called, appropriately, Luck Island. No one lives there, it's just a grassy islet with a few trees, and a tiny beach. You can drop anchor quite close to it and swim in, or even wade in at some hours. It's well known around here as a perfect spot for a picnic or anything else requiring peace and privacy. Goddard must have passed it a thousand times."

"You sound as if you were well acquainted with it yourself," Tina said accusingly.

"Oh I haven't been out there for ages. But Luck might have beckoned to Goddard."

"Can't we go out there now, and take a look?" Tina urged.

Tony considered this for a moment. "No use trying to sail out. What breeze there is is against us and the tide is coming in, too. It would take us hours. The launch being out of commission is tough luck. I could 'borrow' a motor boat, of course."

"Oh, do," Tina begged.

"I suppose you want to come along?" he asked.

"Please. I couldn't stand waiting here alone."

"Okay. Besides, if they are out there, maybe it'll be better to have you with me."

"What do you mean?" Tina asked.

"Well, you are a woman. I don't know what's wrong, but since Maria may be there too, I think you could be useful." It was Tina's turn to be thoughtful. Then Tony tossed her a sweatshirt and a windbreaker. "If you're coming, put these on. It'll be freezing out on the water."

He found some extra garments for himself while Tina bundled into those he'd thrown her. He procured an extra flashlight for her and, taking a lantern, some blankets, and a first-aid kit, he led the way to what seemed to Tina a very small motor boat tied up to one of the pilings of the dock.

"Are we going out on the ocean in this?" she asked in a scared voice.

Tony laughed. "This is a Boston Whaler," he informed her.

"A Whaler?" she repeated in surprise. "This little thing?"

"Not a whaling ship. But it is called a Whaler. It's small but practically unsinkable. Even cut in half, each half floats. So don't worry. Just let me check the tanks to see if they're full. One thing you can say about these stinkpots is that they'll get you there regardless of wind or tide. But it'll be bouncy." He dropped lightly into the boat and held up his hand to assist her. The small craft, to Tina's eyes, was rising and falling uninvitingly, even tied up at the dock. She moved toward the plank seat at the stern of the boat, but Tony motioned her to sit next to him. "If you sit at that end you'll be saddle sore." He arranged the blankets under and around them, then loosed the rope, and pulling the tiller hard to the left, gave the starter a few hard jerks. It caught, and they set out across the harbor.

At first, Tony peered intently into the blackness as they moved out on a zigzagging course to avoid the moored boats, but once clear, he let the engine out full and the bow seemed to rise almost vertically while their end of the boat sank down alarmingly low in the water. Tina's stomach, likewise, rose and fell as they hit each crest of long swell sweeping toward the island and then smacked down into each trough. "We'll be turning as soon as we're clear of the sand bar. It will be smoother then," Tony called reassuringly into her ear, over the din of the motor. As he'd promised, they turned, after passing a flashing buoy, and headed out into the darkness of open water. The moon picked out the crests of small waves, but otherwise they were entirely alone in a black vacuum. The noise of the engine had abated slightly, although it continued to emit a raucous roar. Tony put one arm around her. "Cold?" he asked.

Tina shook her head. "How do you know where you're going?"

Tony grinned at her. "If Goddard's been past Luck Island a thousand times, then make it ten thousand for me. Don't worry. I set my course when we passed the buoy. Besides, I used to know my way there pretty well, at one time."

Tina looked back at him. "But not recently?"

"Not very recently. I couldn't find anyone to keep me company." He paused. "Now why didn't *I* think of Maria?"

She looked at him indignantly, then saw that he was teasing her. "Well, I wish you had," she rejoined. "Then we wouldn't be out here looking for Goddard."

"Do you really?" he asked.

"No," she answered, truthfully. "But will you please stop trying to get a rise out of me?"

Tony laughed. "Well, it's good for my ego, and it did take your mind off your worries, didn't it?" Then, after a moment, he continued, "You'd better switch on the lantern. I know where we're going but we shouldn't take a chance on there being any traffic. If another boat should be in the vicinity, they may not see us if we aren't showing a light. We don't want to be run down." This possibility hadn't previously occurred to Tina. Hurriedly, she switched on the lantern, which produced a narrow but intense beam of white light. Though she peered anxiously about them, there was nothing to be seen but a vast expanse of dark water. Gradually, she began to adjust to the monotonous swaying of the boat, her strained eyes shut, and, leaning against Tony, she slept.

Tina was unsure whether mere minutes or hours had passed when Tony aroused her. "Are we there?" she asked as she saw unrelieved blackness all around.

"Yes, this is Luck," he replied, cutting the engine. "Flash the lantern over to the left." Tina did so, and they were rewarded by the sight of the bare mast of a sailboat; it was anchored near them but far off the shore of what she could dimly make out to be an island by the ruffle of white waves which seemed to trace a horizontal line across the water.

"But why is it anchored way out here?" she asked.

"I don't know. Even if Goddard anchored at low tide, he should have been able to bring her in closer than this. They'll have quite a swim for her from the island. Maybe that's the problem. I'll bet you Maria can't swim and they're stuck on Luck, waiting to be picked up. Although I can't understand how he could be so dumb as to anchor so far out."

They had come several yards closer to the obscure shape of the sailboat as Tony spoke. Peering through the dark, he announced with dismay, "Good God. That's not a Bullseye. It's a big job—a yawl. Although I still can't imagine why anyone should have anchored way out here. And they should be showing lights."

"Not a Bullseye?" Tina echoed. "You mean, Goddard's not out here after all?"

Tony let the engine idle as he considered. They drifted with a bobbing motion over the inky waves, borne slowly closer to the unknown yacht. To Tina's uninformed eyes, the sight of the darkened and apparently abandoned yacht anchored where they had hoped to find Goddard's small craft was ominous.

"Tony," she said nervously, "aren't we coming too close? Shouldn't we head back to the island?"

He did not answer her immediately; he was following

his own line of thought. Finally he told her, "Look, Tina, you stay on the whaler and hold her alongside. I'm going to board the yacht."

"Tony, no," Tina begged. "What if there are people downstairs sleeping? How will you explain? And why should we take the time when we've still got to find Goddard?"

Tony's expression was grim. "I just hope it is a total waste of time."

They drew abreast of the sailboat. After tying their line to the sailboat's cable, Tony stood precariously on the seat of the motor boat and pulled himself up and over the looming side of the yacht. Tina handed up the lantern when he called for it. After a brief time, he dropped back into their boat, untied the line and set off at low speed for the tiny beach of Luck Island.

"Nothing and no one," he explained curtly. "I'm going to check on the island."

Tina exclaimed, "Do we have to? I mean, we come out here looking for Goddard, and when we do find a sailboat, it's deserted and it's not Goddard's at all. Should we really go any further?" She shivered, only partly with cold. "I'm frightened."

"We've come this far; we might as well see who's on the island. I don't suppose there'll be anything worse than a little embarrassment. We can always say we came out for a romantic interlude too, if we're interrupting some couple. But I would have sworn that we'd find your brother here with Maria. I'm not going to turn around and go back without investigating some more."

"But what if the island's just deserted?"

"Someone had better be there," he told her. "Otherwise, what's this empty yacht doing out here? Now be quiet. We're almost there."

In a few minutes he cut the engine again, and they drifted almost onto the beach. Tony stepped out of the boat into hip deep water and began to pull it up onto the beach. Quickly, Tina followed suit, and they soon had their small motor boat safely beached. Tony flashed the lantern around the desolate pebbly shore.

Then Tina started as she heard a wailing moan, choking off into a sob, followed by another. The sounds were coming out of the thick underbrush shadowed by a few scanty trees. She clutched Tony. "My God. What's that awful noise?" she whispered. As they stood immobile, listening intently, they heard a crashing sound coming toward them. In a few seconds the beam of the lantern showed them the forlorn figure of Goddard Mallard. As he peered into the harsh ray of light, Tina saw that he was shivering with cold, stripped to the waist, his cheeks grimy with runnels of tears showing through streaks of dirt.

"You've got to help us," he called. "You can't leave us here. We need help."

Tony thrust the light at Tina and ran to him. "It's me, Tony. What's happened?"

"Thank God! Tony, thank God you've come! I thought they were back again—they took my boat and left us here. Maria's in awful shape. We've got to get her off the island." He stopped, trying to choke back sobs.

Tina ran to him, stripping off her sweatshirt and windbreaker. "You're freezing. Here put these on, Goddard."

He looked at her, puzzled, but after once shaking his head hurried to put on the warm clothing.

"Now, where's Maria?"

"She's back there," he gestured. "I gave her my shirt, sweater, and jacket, and got her to go under the trees to keep warm. I'm afraid she's going to be awfully sick."

"But what happened?" Tina almost screamed at him. Then, without waiting for his answer, Tina and Tony both ran in the direction Goddard had indicated. They found Maria huddled on the ground a few steps under the trees, lying half covered by Goddard's sweater and windbreaker, uttering little wailing sobs. As the light played on her, the reason for her misery was apparent.

Her normally fair, pink-and-white complexion was a deep, unpleasant scarlet, reminding Tina inappropriately of boiled lobster, her eyes were swollen into slits, her lips covered with yellow blisters. One bare red shoulder lay uncovered by the heap of clothing piled on her, disclosing the gaily printed strap of a bathing suit. Her legs were drawn up, and brightly painted toenails decorated her swollen feet.

Tony looked at Goddard and shook his head. "My God, she's parboiled. Why in hell, if you had to take her out sailing, did you let her go dressed like that?"

Goddard swallowed miserably. "I didn't think. She never would meet me even when I offered to take her out on my boat, and then yesterday she said she'd come. When she showed up in that little bikini, well she looked so great, I never thought about it. I just wanted to get away before she changed her mind. It never dawned on me she'd burn up like that. I mean, gee, I never get burned and I'm out every day." Tony forebore from pointing out to him that nothing else could have been expected once Maria's blond fairness was exposed for several hours to bright sunlight not only beating down from overhead but reflected back from the water about them. Goddard continued: "By the time we got here, she looked a little red. And she said she had a headache and wasn't feeling too good, but I figured she'd pick up once she got into the shade. The tide was going out then, and I helped her wade on shore. Then, just when I figured things were going to be all right, she got sick, and she's been groaning and shivering like that for hours. Then they came, but they wouldn't help us. They took my boat and left theirs riding way off shore."

"Who did?" Tony asked.

Tina added, "And why? Why would anyone do such a thing?"

Goddard hesitated. Tony addressed him grimly. "What's going on? You know something, Goddard. You might as well come out with it. You can trust us. What kind of trouble have you gotten yourself mixed up in?"

Goddard swallowed, and turned his face toward Tony pleadingly. "It was just this once, Tony. Try to understand. Maria wanted to meet these guys out here, to pick up a package. One of the other fellows used to do it for her, but he couldn't get his boat today. His parents wanted to use it this weekend. Finally, today, when Maria said she'd come out with me, I didn't see why not. I mean there's never been any trouble before."

"Go on," Tony commanded.

"We were going to pick up some grass and bring it back to the island. Tonight's the big party night and lots of kids would want some. Maria had never come out to Luck before to make the pickup herself, but she didn't think they'd trust me—they didn't know me, and she thought she'd better come along. Only, when they saw what a mess she was in they were furious."

"But why did they take your boat and leave you here?" Tina was impelled to ask.

"They said they'd take it in themselves, but they didn't want to use their own boat, because it's so noticeable. Another Bullseye around here doesn't cause any comment, but a 10-meter yawl is pretty spectacular. Someone might remember her if she came into the harbor. They were supposed to come back for us. I thought you were them."

Tony queried, "You mean they may be back here at any time?"

"They promised they'd come back for us."

Tina interposed, "But who are they? I mean who are these people. Are they gangsters?"

Goddard shook his head. "Oh, gosh no. They're just doing it for the summer until they go back to college. They have a route and make deliveries to all the summer colonies. Someone comes out by boat and picks it up. They're not criminals or anything."

Tina stared at him incredulously. "Not criminals? When they supply an illegal drug, for money, to all the kids on the island and dozens of other places, too. Something's wrong with your head, Goddard."

Tony interrupted her scolding. "Tina's right. Whatever's been going on, take it from me Goddard, you've gotten yourself mixed up in a crime. And they must be pretty callous to leave Maria and you on Luck even if they do mean to come back for you. I don't think we'd better wait for them here."

"What are we going to do, Tony?" Tina asked.

"The first thing is to get Maria into the Whaler. I don't suppose she can walk."

Goddard shook his head. "No. I thought of trying to get her out to their boat, but the backs of her legs are all burned and she just can't move. All I could do was to try and keep her warm."

"Tina, get the blankets," said Tony. "I think we can roll her into one and together we can carry her to the Whaler."

Careful and gentle as they tried to be, the brief trip back to the little beach with Maria slung in the improvised hammock was slow and arduous. They lowered her into the Whaler, Tina sat on the floor of the boat holding Maria's head in her lap. Tony and Goddard managed to launch the little boat into the water, but with the four of them in her, the Whaler was heavily laden.

"Don't use your flashlight now, Tina," Tony reminded her. "I'm going to run the engine on low, to cut the noise. I don't want to give any sign of our presence right now."

"Are we going to steal their yawl?" Goddard asked excitedly. "It would serve them right, after all. I told them they were rotten to leave us out on Luck Island like that."

"Shut up," Tony snapped. "It still hasn't occurred to you that you're in trouble. The last thing we want is to end up with their yawl. If it's too noticeable for them, it's far too noticeable for us. The Coast Guard may have it under observation already for all we know. What we want is to get back your Bullseye and then to get you back home and keep you out of this mess altogether. And, if possible, without having a confrontation with Maria's chums. I don't trust that carefree college-boys story."

"But how are we going to be able to manage that?" Tina asked.

"They'll be coming back to get their yawl, never fear. Whether or not they're planning to rescue Goddard and Maria, I don't know. If they do go on shore, it'll be easier. If not, we still have a chance. But they mustn't see us when they sail in. The Whaler's riding so low in the water, there's a good chance they won't notice her. I'll try to keep the yawl between us and the Bullseye. But first, I want to make sure they can't overtake us, once they're back on board her."

Tina watched as the Whaler was again tied up to the cable by which the big sailboat was anchored. Once more, Tony heaved himself over her side. Tina was thankful that his plan had not required that they transship. She didn't see how they ever could have managed to haul Maria's dead weight from the Whaler bobbing low in the water up and over the sheer sides of the larger boat. Maria, her head sunk in Tina's lap, had mercifully lapsed into semi-consciousness. She occasionally emitted a low groan as the motion of the Whaler, tied up to the cable, caused her discomfort. Goddard had subsided into silence. Tony's admonitions were having effect, Tina hoped.

This time there was quite a wait before Tony returned, but when he again descended into the Whaler he explained in a hushed voice what he had been up to. "I've left them with only a couple of ounces of fuel in the tank, enough so she'll start if they use the engine, but I'm hoping they'll run out before they've made a quarter of a mile."

Goddard exclaimed, "But if we're in the Bullseye and they come after us, they'll outsail us. They can put up enough canvas to overtake us at will."

Tony added, "I hope I've taken care of that too. Now, quiet. Our voices carry over water, and if they're coming in on the Bullseye at any moment, we've got to stay absolutely silent."

They waited in the darkness with waves slapping against the sides of the Whaler making the only sound. Tina hoped that their noise would cover Maria's occasional moans. The blankets were under and around Maria, and all three of them were beginning to shiver as they tried to stay motionless, their ears alert for the least sound of the Bullseye's return.

After an endless wait Goddard began to whisper, "What if they're not coming back tonight after all?"

Tony hushed him. "They've got to. If they have a route, this extra delivery will already have put them behind schedule. They'll have to come back soon."

Even as he finished, they picked up voices, two of them, coming cheerfully toward them out of the night. The Bullseye was approaching and her crew was unsuspecting. As silently as he could, Tony rose and hauled on the line which attached them to the yawl's cable, thrusting the Whaler to the other side of the big sailboat. They remained hidden by its bulk as the Bullseye approached and anchored close to the yawl. They could hear perfectly.

"I think we should get them off Luck. Someone will be out looking for them at daybreak. We'll never make it back to harbor by then. We can't risk being picked up until we've finished making deliveries. The kid has seen us and he'll talk."

"Mike, I told you. Leave them on the island. We can set the Bullseye adrift. It'll be hours before they're found, maybe days. The Coast Guard will pick up the empty boat. They won't have any reason to check Luck Island. We'll have plenty of time."

"Someone else might come out. It's Labor Day. Plenty of people use this as a picnic spot. It's too risky."

"Even if we wanted to, how're we going to get them onto the Bullseye? The kid could swim for it, but Maria'd never make it. We've got no choice."

"Well, I don't like it. It's leaving too much to chance. They might be found too soon. Then, again, they might not be found until too late. We don't want them to die."

"Oh, if that's what you're worried about, you can phone the Coast Guard tomorrow. We'll be safe enough by then. Just tell them to search Luck Island and hang up."

"I guess I could do that."

"Sure. Don't worry so much about them. If Maria hadn't been such a fool this would never have happened. She was never supposed to come out to Luck herself, just to send someone to make a pickup. It's worked all summer. Why did she have to flub it up now? Anyway, the important thing is to get rid of the stuff and the money, and get the yawl home before the kid can talk."

"Okay."

Tina could hear the sound of footsteps on the yawl's deck. The anchor was being pulled up. Quickly Tony untied the rope by which the Whaler was held in the yawl's shadow. Tina held her breath, fearing their imminent discovery. The least glance over the yawl's side would disclose them, huddled in the Whaler. Then what would happen? She was relieved to hear the yacht's engine start. It was a good thing that Mike and his companion were in a hurry. If they'd only leave now, Tony's plan might work.

For a moment it seemed that it would. The Bullseye

was left adrift and the yawl began to pull away. Then the Whaler, caught in the yawl's wash, began to bump against her side. Frantically, Tony and Goddard leaned far forward, trying to thrust her clear. It was too late.

"What's that noise, Mike?"

"I dunno, Steve. I got the anchor in all right. Let me go aft and check it."

Tina held her breath.

"Jesus Christ!"

They had been spotted. Tony leaped for the starter of the Whaler and jerked at it hard while he pulled at the tiller. The Whaler jumped away from the big 10-meter's side even as Mike screamed at Steve, "It's a little motor boat! They've been tied up alongside us. Let the engine out full."

Tina could see Steve looking down over the side at them as they spurted past, but the advantage of surprise would soon be lost. Steve had obviously had the same thought. They heard the vibration of the yawl's powerful engines as it came about. Tony glanced back over his shoulder, appraising their chances. Tina could see him calculating. They could dodge their pursuers by taking the little Whaler into shallow waters, where the yawl could not follow but then they would run the risk of being penned up on Luck. Or they could try to escape from her by bobbing and weaving until the larger vessel ran out of gas. His decision was soon made. He pulled at the tiller again, sending the Whaler off on a new course but still out to sea. The yawl, pursuing, turned too, but not soon enough. As soon as it began to come about to intercept the little Whaler on her new course, Tony again shifted direction. But, this way they were being driven around a circle, and would ultimately be pointed back at Luck Island. On the next change of course, Tony pointed his little craft back, reversing the twenty degree turn they had just taken. If luck was with him, the yawl would fail to pick up his change of direction in time, and the rush of her engines would carry the larger craft past the Whaler, inland of them.

It almost worked. The yawl too had changed direction but not quite enough. Tina held back a scream as the looming sides swept down on them. For an instant it appeared that the Whaler would be left behind, in the clear, but before they were quite safe, the starboard hull of the yawl dealt the Whaler a smashing blow. Then it was past. Goddard and Tina exchanged looks of dismay. A portion of the stern section of their tiny boat had disappeared, dropped off into the water.

Tony eyed his damaged craft grimly. "I hope what they said about these jobs is right. We're going to find out." He turned the Whaler slowly, setting a course away from Luck Island. The yawl turned too. This time it appeared that she would run them down. Tina closed her eyes. The roar of the yawl's engine grew louder, and then, in answer to her prayers, subsided, choked, and died away.

"They're adrift!" Goddard yelled.

Tony nodded. "Thank God I didn't leave them any more gas. But they'll raise sail and come after us in a few minutes, when they figure out what's happened to the engine. This next part's going to be a little tricky." He held the Whaler steady for a few more minutes, then cut the engine. "Goddard, Tina, keep a good look out ahead."

"What are we looking for now?" Tina asked.

"The Bullseye, of course. She should be drifting right around here."

A few minutes proved him right. They picked out the small sailboat which was rolling forlornly in the water to their left.

"Goddard, I'm going to come up next to her. I want you to go on board and sail her back to the Yacht Club. Do you think you're up to it?"

"Sure, Tony. But what about you? Now that we've

found her, aren't you going to come on board too? With the Whaler's stern stove in, she may sink under you. You'd all better leave the Whaler and come on board with me."

Tony considered. He turned to Tina. "What about it? You can go on board with Goddard and get back. You'd better run without lights, but you'll have a good chance of making it, if you two start right now."

"But what about you and Maria?" Tina asked. "Aren't you coming too?"

Tony laughed. "I don't want to abandon ship—particularly when it's not even mine. I borrowed this boat, and I'd better make an effort to bring it back in, even if it does have a piece missing. Besides, if I run before them in the Whaler, they'll follow the sound of my engine, and leave you alone."

"You can't do it, Tony. The Whaler will take on water. You'll sink," Tina whispered.

"Make your mind up quickly, Tina. I'm going to chance it. I want Goddard to get his boat back to the island. But I'm going to make for the Coast Guard station at Haddon, with Maria. They'll get her to a doctor. I ought to be able to stay ahead of the yacht. They don't know it yet, but they're going to have a hard time with their sails."

Goddard asked, "Are you sure you fixed them?"

"I hope so. Quick, Tina. Go with Goddard or come with me."

"I'll stay with you. Just as long as you think Goddard will be all right."

"He ought to be. Okay, then, Goddard, jump for it, and get back home as fast as you can. Leave the rest to us."

Goddard scrambled on board. They waited to make sure the Bullseye had been left in sailing order. Then, with a brief wave, Tony started the Whaler's tiny motor again and they roared away from the Bullseye.

Tina shifted closer to Tony's feet, but he stopped her. "We're taking on a little water, but don't worry. Goddard's room is going to be more appreciated than his company. His absence has lightened us. We ought to make it. I hope they don't go after Goddard. I'm letting the engine out full. They ought to be coming after us now and I want to make sure they can hear us."

It seemed to Tina that that was a certainty; the noise of their engine was a roar in her ears, precluding any further questions. She could only hope that Tony was right, about everything.

Glancing in back of them desperately she didn't know whether she was glad or not when she saw the pale canvas sails of the yawl coming toward them. Tony had been correct in his guess; they'd forgotten the Bullseye, or chosen to pursue the Whaler. But it seemed certain that the yawl would be able to sail them down. The sea was calm, and only a light breeze was blowing, but with the spread of canvas they had hoisted, the 10-meter was making good speed through the light seas. The Whaler was hampered by the water which she had shipped, and which still entered and ebbed through the hole in the stern. They must have at least three miles to go to the Coast Guard station; it seemed impossible that they could make it.

Tina looked around at Tony. To her amazement, he was grinning. "What's there to smile about?" she shouted at him.

He heard her the second time and laughed. "All we need is a good puff of wind. I wish we could be close enough to see their faces."

"What?" she screamed back.

"Wind. Just pray for a little gust of wind."

Tina eyed the yawl, now definitely drawing up on them. "You're crazy," she yelled. "They're overhauling us now. More wind will only help them."

"Pray for it anyway," was the answering cry.

Tina could make out the yawl's hull, and the yellow stripe painted around it, before their prayer was answered. The yawl was close enough to them for Tina and Tony to follow what was happening. The jenny bellied out under the pressure of the breeze, a line parted, and the sail drooped, sagging slack. The boom whirled around and fouled the other lines. The yawl yawed crazily, and presented her side to them. She could make out the figures of two men, scrambling to free the lines, then heard a splintering crack.

Tony shouted, "Better than I could have hoped. They're dismasted. We're home free—if we can make it."

Tina breathed deeply. "You mean you knew that would happen all the time?"

Tony nodded. "Well, I hoped on slowing them down, anyway. I couldn't count on their letting themselves be dismasted. I fixed it when I went on board. I frayed the lines. All we needed was that little extra strain on the jenny caused by a stiff bit of breeze, and we got it."

Tina gazed down at the limp figure wrapped in damp blankets still cradled in her lap. "Tony, what are we going to do now? What about Maria? You don't think that she'll die, or anything?" Tina finally voiced the fear that was in her thoughts.

"Nope. She's not all that badly burned. Your idiot brother at least had the sense to get her out of the sun before she turned crisp. But she sure won't be feeling any too good for a week or so." He added, "It's no more than she deserves after all. She shouldn't have been so greedy and she should never have let a kid like Goddard get involved. My God, Tina, you should be delighted to see her put out of action. What with one extracurricular activity and another, the girl's responsible for what practically amounts to a one-woman crime wave on our secluded little island. I just hope that once we've gotten her to a doctor, we'll have seen the last of her."

The nightmarish trip stretched on. The sky was beginning to lighten to a mauve-gray which outlined the mainland. Tina's arms and legs ached; she knew Tony must be as weary as she was. He turned the boat north, and it was with unutterable relief that they finally made out the white tower of the Coast Guard lighthouse at Haddon.

Soon after they had docked and reported themselves to the officer in charge, an ambulance rolled onto the wharf. With the assistance of the attendant they were able to transfer Maria from the Whaler to the ambulance. Tina was assured that the girl's condition, while temporarily painful, should not prove very serious. Without hesitation, Tina committed the Hemmingways to pay for Maria's hospital stay. She was quite certain that the funds would be forthcoming. Then she and Tony, after calling off the search for Goddard, reported that they had passed a dismasted yawl somewhere near Luck Island. The Coast Guard officer promised that they would render the boat prompt assistance. Tony and Tina had agreed to say no more. There was no doubt in their minds that the Coast Guard's search for the yawl would be followed by its swift apprehension. Once the boat and its crew were picked up and identified they would just have to hope that Goddard would not be implicated. And, as Tony had said to her in securing her agreement to silence, "If we aren't going to complain about her running us down, everything else is just hearsay. We don't actually *know* anything about their marijuana route. It's just what Goddard said. We sure don't want to bring him into this. We couldn't even identify Mike and Steve. We really don't have any facts to furnish. But I can't imagine that they'll get away without having to give some explanations. I don't think their marijuana route will ever be resumed. Anyway, right now I'm beat. Let's get back home as soon as we can, and let things sort themselves out later."

Tina was too tired to debate the point.

Confronted once more with a descent into the leaking Whaler, she almost balked. "I really don't know if I can face another trip in that thing," she sighed wearily.

"You're just worn out. Look, it's light now. I'll have us back on the island in less than an hour. Then you can relax and get some sleep." Too tired to argue, Tina meekly gave him her hand and settled herself against him as they set forth again.

This trip was made in silence, and it was with infinite gratitude that Tina set eyes on the island, then the harbor, then the Yacht Club once again. As they neared the dock, Tony pointed out Goddard's boat to her, safe at its mooring, and her remaining fear was allayed.

"I guess he's gotten home by now, and everyone's calmed down. I can't imagine what he's thought up to tell the girls, can you?" Tina couldn't help speculating.

"Let him worry about that, Tina. You've worried about Goddard enough for one night."

"Oh, but if I'd shown more concern for him before this, it might never have happened."

Tony stared at her with a bemused expression. "Do you mean that you're prepared to shoulder the blame for this whole incident? What about Goddard himself, or Lilly, or his stepfather for that matter?"

"But, Tony, I was here. He was my responsibility."

He groaned. "Tina, Tina, don't always be taking on other people's responsibilities. Don't you find it a burden to have them all relying on you? You invite it, I swear you do. You open your eyes wide, look out brimming with sympathy, asking if there isn't some way you can be of help. Of course people take advantage. Who wouldn't? There you are—like some sort of Girl Scout, radiating honesty and intelligence, all ready to be trusted. You've got a life of your own to lead, you know, if you can ever make the time for it."

Tina nodded. "I suppose you might be right. My besetting sin is the need to understand, and once I know, of course I want to help."

"Oh, of course," Tony agreed. "Very praiseworthy. But can't you exercise a bit of restraint in the future? Be a little more selective in the choice of those who are to be the objects of your solicitude? Maybe narrow it down to just one?"

Tina looked up at him for further enlightenment. The boat bumped gently against a timber supporting the dock. Their endless ride was at last over.

Tony tied the damaged Whaler to the timber and helped Tina out of the boat. She left it without any reluctance.

"Ugh. I never want to go out in a boat again."

Tony laughed. "It's been pretty awful, I agree. But that's just a stinkpot. When I take you sailing on my Star, you'll see what it's all about."

The indefinite invitation remained dangling in the air. Glancing over toward the parked Volkswagen, Tony asked her, "Do you feel that you have to rush right home to check up on everyone, or shall we go inside for a while? I can make us some coffee."

Tina didn't hesitate. "I'd much rather come inside with you. We can start off the Labor Day holiday together. I think we deserve it."

Chapter 18

The sight of her reflection in the mirror of the Yacht Club ladies' room was enough to stir Tina to activity. Here was no pretension to glamour; she barely looked civilized. She used the comb and brush which she found lying on the counter, but even her most vigorous efforts were unavailing. Her hair, soaked with salt spray, had developed a mind of its own and stood out about her face in a dark, curling halo. She washed the salt-stiffened skin of her face, and rinsed it with icy water until she felt alert again. But, without makeup, she could not attempt allure. Circumstances had resurrected the old Tina. Perforce, the healthy, outdoor look of her own naked face would have to do. With a sigh, she finally gave up and rejoined Tony. While she had been trying to improve her appearance, he had been able not only to wash up but also to produce a hot mug of indifferent coffee to set before her.

"This is my last day on the island," Tina said reflectively, as she sipped the hot but tasteless fluid from the mug. "Yesterday, I couldn't wait for this summer to be over, but, somehow, right now, I wish it wasn't all coming to an end quite yet."

"I'll be staying on for another week or so. I don't go back to Dartmouth until then," Tony replied. "Once the crowd clears out after Labor Day, the island is really nice. Why don't you stay on too?"

"I have to take the kids into town and dispatch them to their schools. I promised Lilly I would."

"You certainly earn your keep as far as she's concerned," Tony remarked dryly. "She really has perfected the knack of putting people to use."

"Don't we all?" Tina replied.

"Well, let's just say that with Lilly it's more highly developed. When does school start for you, Tina?"

"In ten days. I'll be able to finish this semester, anyway."

"Aren't you going to complete your last year?" he asked.

"I'll probably have to get a job and finish up later, unless I can wangle a scholarship-loan. They aren't too plentiful in my field though. My trust money stops in December when I'm twenty-one."

Tony laughed. "That's when mine started, last year."

"Do you mean you've been working all summer even though you've an income of your own?" Tina asked.

"Oh, I let it pile up. It doesn't do me any harm to have a job. Say, why don't you let me lend you the money you need—for school. It doesn't seem fair that you should have to scrape for it."

Tina looked at him with indignation. "Well, aren't you generous. No, thanks. That would be using you, with a vengeance."

"You could pay it back. Besides, I wouldn't call that using me. After all, I offered. And when someone offers to do something, for a girl he likes I mean, I wouldn't call accepting it 'using' the person."

"Oh? What would you call it then?" she countered stiffly.

"It depends, doesn't it, on how the people felt about each other." He continued slowly, "If they were in love, for example, I'd call it sharing."

Tina looked into his eyes and he held her gaze steadily. "But, that assumes that the people were in love." There was a pause. Then she asserted, "We're not."

He took the mug from her hands and gently placed it on the floor beside them. Then, slowly, he took her into his arms and kissed her. They stayed locked for a few minutes, neither wanting to end the embrace. Tony murmured into her ear, "Are you sure?"

Tina thrust herself out of his arms. "Is this another come on? You've been trying to make me all summer, haven't you? I thought you'd finally given it up."

"This is different. It's not just that I want to seduce you anymore. Now I do know you, and I think we could love each other. Don't fight against me so hard. Let yourself love me. I think you already do, a little, in spite of yourself."

Tina did not deny it. But she protested, "I don't think I want to be in love, with anyone. Lilly's in love, with that egocentric Findlay Hemmingway, and it makes her behave in the most awful way."

"That's Lilly. I'd say she was as much in love with herself as she is with Hemmingway. Being in love doesn't change a person's whole nature. It makes them more themselves, if you understand me. And it's you— you yourself Tina, that I'm in love with."

"Did you know that your mother has her own plans for me?" Tina inquired with a smile. "She thinks that Charles should fall in love with me, and we should get married."

"My mother said that?" Tony was surprised and amused. "A schemer with a lead thumb, I'd say. You and Charles? That's ridiculous, you know."

Tina nodded thoughtfully. "Yes, it is really, isn't it. It sounded very attractive at first. But, although I can admire Charles, there isn't really any reason why he should fall in love with me or why I should fall in love with him. We've nothing in common, at all."

"Of course it's ridiculous. He's my own brother, and he's handsome as a god and good-natured too, but he's all surface. He could never appreciate you. He'll find someone to marry sooner or later, and they'll have lots of little kids and entertain charmingly all winter in town, all summer on the island. That's not for you, Tina."

"It sounds kind of sweet and cozy, doesn't it? But you're right. I could never fall in love with him and live that kind of life," Tina agreed.

"You're too intelligent for that. And, if you'll forgive my modesty, so am I. I'm going to go through medical school, and you're going to have a career in archaeology. I wouldn't want you to give up your whole life before you've begun."

"Then, what exactly is it that you do want, Tony?" she asked shyly.

"Just for us to love each other. No. I don't just mean to make love once, and then forget it. I mean we'll see each other, whenever we can, we'll share together and plan together. We might even get married, if that's the only way you'll take money from me. But we wouldn't settle down into being a couple. We'd each go on with our own lives too."

Tina smiled at him. "You've got it all thought out, haven't you?"

"This isn't just impulse, Tina. I've had a lot of time to think about you—all summer, and then all through last night. I'm right, aren't I? You love me, too."

Tina shook her head. "I'm not sure, Tony. I don't have it all thought out, like you. I don't know. Maybe I will, some day. Maybe I do. I can't be sure of anything."

He kissed her again. Her arms tightened about him. The warmth of his body, the strength of his arms, the salty fragrance of his hair and skin, enveloped her totally. Their lips merged, their tongues tested, tasted. Tina let her hand caress his neck, his hair. With her eyes closed, she let herself know him with all of her senses at once. When he released her, she still clung to his embrace.

"Maybe?" he teased, gently.

"Yes," she answered. "Oh, Tony, I didn't know."

"Hush." he said. "Don't talk. I'll take you home now. I've got to work today. It's Labor Day, and people will be coming in soon."

She nodded.

"I'll come for you tonight, as soon as I can lock up here."

"For a walk on the beach?" she asked, with a little laugh.

"No, not for a walk on the beach, my girl. That was never a very good idea. Much too gritty and not enough privacy. No, I'll take you out on my boat for a sail. We'll get clear of the harbor, and drop anchor where we'll be all alone, and we'll make love."

"Aren't you planning to take me to Luck Island?" Tina asked, teasing him.

Tony grinned at her. "No, I won't take you to Luck Island. I won't need that sort of luck, will I? I'll come back to the city and we'll spend some time together before we start school, and we'll have weekends and vacations until the summer. I can take you to Mexico then, and we'll have the rest of our lives together."

"And we won't come back to the island?" Tina asked.

"Never," he answered. "We'll never have to come back here."

Tina chuckled. "Well, not for years, maybe. But, of course, we'll be back for the christening of our first child."

Tony laughed. "Yes, we'll probably come back then."
Then, seriously, he asked her, "Will you come, Tina?
Will you come sailing with me?"

She answered as soberly as he, "Yes, Tony. Yes, I
will."